Sacrifice

Wendy Zuccarello

Published by Wendy Zuccarello, 2023.

This is a work of fiction. Similarities to real people, places, or events are entirely coincidental.

SACRIFICE

First edition. February 1, 2023.

Copyright © 2023 Wendy Zuccarello.

ISBN: 979-8224995790

Written by Wendy Zuccarello.

Table of Contents

*To my son, AJ, who is always a good sounding board for my ideas.
He also came up with the name of this book! Thanks, buddy!*

P*ain.*

Screaming.

Agony.

I am aware of every part of my body simply because it all hurts. There is pain, radiating up and down my arms and legs, my head is throbbing, and my skin feels like it is on fire. I know exactly where I am, and that scares the shit out of me.

There is a snickering to my right.

"Stop," a voice says. "Give her a few minutes to recover and then hit her again."

I know that voice. It's the voice of my nightmares. Dr. Garrett Anderson. The one who tortured and beat me when I was at the facility with Cooper. That was months ago, but somehow, I am back here.

"Please don't do this," I hear myself say. My voice sounds weak, and distant.

We must have been doing this for a while because I am exhausted, utterly spent. Torture will do that to you.

"Oh, come now, Miss Daniels. We are just getting started. I told you what would happen if you didn't do what I asked. Then you escaped. Now that I have you back, we are going to have some real fun," Anderson says sadistically.

"You ass hat!"

He smiles, and all I could think was 'oh shit.'

"Hit her again," he shouts.

Pain. This is nothing like the last time. They have me hooked up to some type of battery and they are shocking me. I can't even describe what this feels like. I'm panting, screaming. I feel like I am going to explode. I knew if I came back, he wouldn't hold anything back. I knew what I was walking into. But with everything that has happened, how could I have made any other decision? I had to do this. I had to come back.

"Hold," Anderson says.

There is a long pause. I take the time to catch my breath.

"Now, Miss Daniels. Tell me what I want to know, and I will end this suffering. Where is your base? How many people are there?"

I spit on him.

He raises his hand slowly and wipes the spit away.

"You might as well just kill me now. I will never tell you," I shout.

"Oh, Miss Daniels. I'm not going to kill you. I'm going to break you," he hisses.

He nods at someone behind me, and the pain is instant. I'm screaming through the agony. There is no logical thought, my brain is a jumbled mess. I have no idea how long it lasts. Eventually, it stops, and I am left panting, trying to catch my breath. I relish the freedom from pain.

"You really should have just answered the question, my dear," Anderson says as he raises his hand. He is holding a knife. No, not a knife. A dagger. The most terrifying-looking dagger I have ever seen. "I gave you every opportunity to provide me with the information I need. This is your fault. You asked for this."

I only have a split second to contemplate what he says, before he drives the dagger, right into my chest.

I shoot up in bed, covered in sweat, grasping at my chest. There is no dagger, no Dr. Anderson. I am in bed with Cooper in our room at the barracks. It was just a dream. Just a dream.

"Cass?" Cooper says sleepily, sitting up and rubbing my back. "Baby, what's wrong?"

I break down and cry. That's how real it felt. I felt that dagger go into my chest. I felt the pain of the electrocution.

"I'm fine. Just a bad dream. Go back to sleep," I say weakly.

He pulls me into his arms, the only place that I feel safe anymore. It's been a few months since we came to this base. After Cooper and

I escaped the prison and we made our way to the base, we settled here and called this room our home. It's not much, but we don't need much, just each other. We have spent the last few months traveling around the east coast, taking down the government facilities that are holding women and men hostage, hoping to figure out just what it was that wiped out almost all the female population. We have saved so many. Not just women, but the men that they have imprisoned, too. Our forces are strong, and we have developed a foolproof method of infiltrating the facilities.

I have been having nightmares about my time at that prison since we got here. Up to this point, I have been able to hide them from Cooper. He doesn't need anything else to worry about. I need him to focus on staying safe on each mission, not worrying about my stupid dreams. It seems like just yesterday that we lost everyone. Everyone being my mom and the other billions of women who died suddenly with no explanation. It happened over two waves that hit a few weeks apart. Between those two waves, we lost over seventy-five percent of the female population. My brother Austin and I lost our dad shortly after that when they were trying to protect me. That left us on our own. Austin made plans with his best friend Cooper to meet up at his cabin, but we never made it there. Austin got taken, then I got taken. I thankfully met Cooper in the facility that they took me to, but not until after I was beaten and tortured. We finally escaped, but the damage had already been done – hence, the nightmares.

"Don't push me away, Cass. Talk to me. What's going on in that head of yours?" he asks, pulling me closer to him.

My head is on his shirtless chest, which gives me an excellent view of his perfect body. But unfortunately, all I can think about it how that dream felt.

"Baby," he says, pulling my chin up so that I have to look at him.

A few stray tears run down my cheeks, and he wipes them away with his thumbs. He is holding my face gently. It is the way a man holds the woman he loves.

"Talk to me."

I take a deep breath, palming my chest again. I have pain still, right where the dagger went in. It was so real.

"I was back at the prison with Anderson. He had me on the table and was torturing me for information about this place and our people. It felt so real," I say, pausing to rub my chest again. "I could feel the pain."

He is trying to keep his expression neutral, but I see the anger there, he can't hide it.

He pulls me close to him again. "Cass, there isn't anything I wouldn't do to make all of that go away. I wish you never had to go through that. But don't think for one second that I would ever let you get taken by him again. I would die before I let that happen."

I immediately feel guilty. In the past few months, I have managed not to tell him about the discussion I had with General Mike McConnell and Colonel Steven Walters, the men who run this site. They asked me if I would be willing to go back to Dr. Anderson's facility to get some information from him. Apparently, that facility is different from the rest and would require a lot more recon to take it down. We figured out that his facility is the main site for the government's research. That's off the record of course. The President and his advisors won't recognize that they have anything to do with these facilities. They just say that they are doing everything in their power to take them down. Yet somehow, nothing has been done. The General told me that Anderson was the President's top medical advisor. Not the one that the public was aware of, his "other" top medical advisor. The one who participated in questionable research, who was willing to do just about anything the President asked. I would have never known this if I weren't here. It was something only the higher-ups knew. Now that I am part of what some have begun to call the Cause, I am privy to certain classified information.

"Cass. I promise. You will never see him again," I am jerked out of my head when Cooper speaks.

"I know, Coop. I know. It's just that it felt so real. I could physically feel the pain. I felt it when he killed me," I say, trying to explain why I am so upset over just a dream.

"Over my dead body will he ever get his hands on you again," he says in a growl.

"And that's why I love you."

He tilts my chin up so that he can kiss me. I can't imagine where I would be right now if it weren't for Cooper. I'm not only talking about how he fought for me and got me out of that prison and saved my life. No. I'm talking about how this man is my reason for living. He is the love of my life, my soul mate. Whatever you want to call it. I don't even want to think about having to live without him.

Every time we go on a mission, every time we are at a new facility, and I am sitting in that Jeep, waiting for him to come back to me, I worry. Because I honestly don't think I could survive without him.

Our kiss turns heated, and soon we are both naked.

"I love you, Cassidy. And I promise you that you will never be taken away from me again. I won't allow it. I can't. You are my world, my life."

"I love you, Cooper. I love you so much."

Our lovemaking is quick but fierce, both of us trying to convey to the other how much we mean to each other. It's not until after, when I am lying in his arms, that he says the last thing I want to hear right now.

"Cass, I swear to you on my life that I will always protect you. And you know I mean that because I would never lie to you, I would never keep something from you. I will always, always take care of you."

It's at that moment, that exact moment, that I realize, I can never tell Cooper about the deal that I made with the General.

"Wake up, sleepy head," Cooper says sweetly as he nuzzles my neck. We fell back asleep last night after my nightmare. He wrapped himself so tightly around me, making me feel safe. I thankfully slept the rest of the night sans nightmares.

"Five more minutes," I whine. "I don't want to get up yet. I'm too comfortable."

He leans down and kisses my nose. "Nope. We've got a meeting this morning with the General. You know we can't be late. You may not be a soldier officially, but we've got you as close as you can be to one at this point. It's not in our nature to be late."

I growl. "One of these days I'm going to get you to be late for something."

"Oh yeah? And just how would you do that?" he asks, kissing my jaw.

"Wouldn't you like to know?"

He laughs.

We gather our things and head down to the showers. That's probably the only thing I miss at this point. We have our own room, but we still share the showers with the rest of the people on our floor. Not that that stops us from sharing a shower, it would just be nice to not have to worry about other people while we are in there.

We quickly shower and get dressed. As we are leaving our room, my brother Austin is turning the corner at the end of the hall.

"Hey, you two. I was just coming to see if you wanted to grab some chow really quick before the meeting," he says, pulling me into a side hug while rubbing the top of my head with his knuckles. He knows I hate that.

"Stop that," I say, swatting at his hand and elbowing him in the side.

Cooper pulls me back into him and fixes my hair. "You know, you might not want to pick on her anymore. With all the training we've been doing, she just might be able to take you down."

Over the past few months, the boys have focused on getting me in the best shape of my life, while teaching me more about weapons and tactical maneuvers. I have definitely toned up and put on some muscle.

"Yeah," I say, punching Austin in the stomach, which unfortunately is like punching a brick wall. "Ow. That hurt."

"Ha. Kid, you'll never be able to take me in a fight," he says while laughing.

We make our way to the mess hall and grab a quick breakfast. Well, mine is quick. I grab an apple, while the two beastly men that I am with both grab plates full of eggs, bacon, sausage, and some pancakes. I know they are both big guys who require a lot of calories to maintain their bodies, but it always amazes me how much they can put away.

We head over to the administration building where our meeting is to take place. Some of the men we pass stop to salute us. Well, Austin and Cooper. They are both Staff Sergeants in the Marines. Nobody salutes me, I'm nobody. There are quite a few people gathered in the room by the time we get there. Most of them are the usual suspects. The General, the Colonel, their assistants, Al, Simon, and Teddy, or as I like to call them, the Chipmunks, are all there. Once the last person enters the room, the General clears his throat.

"All right. Let's get started," he says firmly.

We all take our seats, me between Cooper and Austin. We are planning our next take down, a facility in New York.

"I have some new information on the facility in upstate New York. All the facilities around the country have been increasing their security recently and I think we are the reason. Our existence is no longer a secret. Word has traveled all the way up to the President about our group, and he is not happy. They know what we are doing, and they are doing everything in their power to protect their research. I wish I could tell you that what they are doing has produced any type of results, but it hasn't. They only thing that they are achieving is the torture and deaths of viable women."

The room falls silent for a minute while the General lets that information sink in. Unfortunately, what happened to me is not quite a secret. I feel all eyes on me as the General looks around the room. Cooper takes my hand and squeezes it reassuringly.

"Now, our next target is in a secluded area, just outside of Utica. We will leave in two days. This will not be a one-day trip this time. We will have to set up camp about sixty miles away to avoid detection. We will attack at night this time. As you know, up to this point, we have done all our work in day light. That is what they now expect. We must catch them off guard. Our intel has told us that there is a guard change at nineteen hundred hours. That is our target time."

The General goes on to map out our attack. Well, their attack. All I ever do is wait in the truck for them to return. I do help with communications. The guy who stays with me at the rendezvous point is a communications specialist and he has been teaching me about the technology that they use. We have a lot more people here now to help with our missions. They have been training anyone who is interested in combat and weapons, all in the hopes of protecting what we have built here.

Since all of this started, society collapsed. We've spent just as much time taking down facilities as we have helping out around in areas that have suffered. We have brought so many people back to the base that we had to have new housing facilities built. Thankfully, we have quite a few people who are skilled in that department who have helped. We gather supplies and bring them back here, and they do the constructing. It is one of the things that I have enjoyed the most. When we would pick up someone who was struggling and bring them here where they have protection, shelter, and food, well, it is very humbling. I spent time on my own back at the beginning, back after Austin was taken, and before I met Cooper. That time on my own was the hardest of my life. Going day to day not knowing where I was going to get my next meal, or whether I was going to have a roof over my head at night was beyond stressful.

The President still claims to be in control of the country, but that is a lie. There is no organization anymore. We are in a situation of every man for himself. People panicked when everything happened. Families were torn apart by the loss of mothers and daughters, wives, and partners. With the facilities popping up all over the country, survival became the main goal. People hid wherever they could to protect those that survived. The threat of another possible event loomed over everyone. Those that are doing legitimate research are frustrated as there is no explanation in site. One day, everything was fine, the next, it wasn't. As much as we want to know what killed over seventy five percent of women, our new goal became stopping Anderson and his lackeys. We should be focusing on rebuilding, not on some psycho with a God complex.

The General continues and my mind begins to wander. I haven't been able to stop thinking about Dr. Anderson and going back in. When General McConnell, or Mike, and Colonel Walters suggested that I accept a secret mission to gather more intel on Anderson, they said it was completely up to me, but is it really? What kind of a person would I be if I didn't do this? They made it very clear that they didn't want to make an attempt at that facility unless they knew more about Anderson's research. And who better to get it than someone who they are using for the experiments?

I know if I do it, if I go back there, I won't be coming back out alive. Once he has his hands on me again, I am done. I don't know why, but

Anderson has some kind of vendetta against me. He will take extreme pleasure in torturing and killing me slowly.

I notice that the room has grown silent, and everyone is looking at me expectantly. Oops.

"Uh... I'm sorry, what was the question?" I ask, embarrassed.

There is a slight chuckle around the room. "I asked if you are ready to run point on communications this time around," Mike asks me.

"Oh. Sure. I can do that," I answer, surprised they are asking me.

"Great. Private Trottman will be with you, but we think you are ready," Mike explains.

He goes back to discussing the plan. Cooper leans over to whisper in my ear.

"You ok?"

I just nod, not sure that I could answer honestly if I had to do anything other than that. Because the truth is, I am as far from ok as I can be. I try to focus on the meeting. Cooper can't stop glancing at me. I know he is worried, and he should be. I feel like the worst person for keeping this from him. But I know that if he knew I was considering doing this, he would do everything in his power to stop me. And I can't let that happen. If I do this, no... when I do this, I have to go all in. I am the one that Anderson wants, no one else. I just wish I knew why.

I think about all the lying that I am going to have to do. Lying to Cooper. Lying to Austin. Lying to myself. I have no idea where I am going to get the courage to go through with this. I feel like this is too much to ask of me. They are asking one person to do this for the good of the rest of the country. I guess in the grand scheme of things, it is worth it.

As I sit here and listen to these brave men, I realize that they have all made sacrifices to be here. I know a few of the men lost their wives and daughters to this... thing. But there are others who brought their families here. Not only for protection but to help in the cause. They are risking their lives, day in and day out, for the greater good. Who am I to say that my life is more valuable than theirs? What kind of person would I be if I turned my back on this mission?

Before I realize it, the meeting is adjourned. Smaller groups break off. Cooper and the Chipmunks are talking about the equipment we will need to take with us when we leave. I look around the room and make eye contact with Mike. He nods his head at me to come over there. I squeeze Cooper's hand.

"Hey. I'm going to ask Mike a question. I'll be right back."

"I'll come with you," he says.

"No!" I shout too quickly and loudly. He narrows his eyes and looks at me, he knows I am up to something, he just doesn't know what.

"What's going on, Cass?"

"Nothing. I just don't want you to stop talking just to come with me to ask a question. I am perfectly capable of walking over to the other side of the room on my own, Coop." I chuckle, trying to make light of everything.

He just stares at me. Crap. He's going to be all questions when we are alone.

"Ok. I'll be right here when you are done," he says, bringing my hand up and kissing the back of it.

I smile at him, trying to convince him that all is ok.

I make my way over to Mike. He dismisses the two soldiers that are in front of him and pulls me out into the hallway.

"Cassidy. How are you?" he asks.

"I'm good, Mike. I was going to come to speak with you, but I am having a hard time getting away from Cooper. He knows I am keeping something from him, and I hate it, to be perfectly honest."

He sighs. "I know. Believe me, I know. It is hard to keep something from those you love. I have had to do it many times over the years in my position. There were many times I was deployed into hostile territories, and I had to keep that from my wife. But it was better for her if she didn't know. Just like it is better for Cooper not to know about this mission."

Mike's wife and two daughters survived the initial waves of this thing. He brought them here to the base. I met them back at the beginning of our time here and see them from time to time.

I just nod. I understand what he is saying, but it doesn't make it any easier.

"I'm assuming that means you have made a decision about the mission," he says.

"Yes. I have." I pause, needing a minute to convince myself one last time that I have no other choice. "I will do it, but I have a stipulation."

"I figured as much," he says, smiling sadly.

"Please don't tell Cooper or Austin about it until it is absolutely necessary. Cooper will lose his mind and come after me, getting himself killed. The main reason I am doing this is so that they have the best possibility of survival once you decide to take down Anderson's facility. If I am going to die," I have to stop to choke back to sob that is threatening its way up my throat. "If I am going to die, they have to know that it was to protect them."

"Cassidy, if you do this, you will not die. We will get there in time to get you out. You will be working directly with Jax. He is the best of the best. He will do everything in his power to protect you." He reaches out and takes my hand. "We will get you out."

I have to bite my tongue. I want to tell him that he's wrong. That once I am in that facility again with Anderson, I will be tortured, beaten, and killed. Oh, make no mistake. Anderson will drag out the torture for as long as possible. There is no way that he will let me live this time. I want to tell Mike that he doesn't have to make any empty promises. I know that this mission is the last one I will ever go on. But I don't say any of that.

"Ok, Mike. I'm in."

"I will be in touch with the details. We have to figure out how we are going to get you away from Cooper without him knowing."

"Please leave that part up to me. If I am going to lie to him and deceive him, I don't want anyone else involved. Let him be mad at me."

We talk about our next mission for a few minutes. I feel someone watching me and look over to see Cooper standing in the doorway. He comes over to me immediately and puts his arm around my waist, kissing me on the top of the head.

"Sorry, I wanted to talk to Mike about his expectations of me on this next trip," I lie easily. It makes me nauseous.

"It's ok, Cass. I just wanted to let the General know that I will go over everything with you before we leave," Coop says.

"I know you will. And I know that Cassidy will do just fine," Mike says, smiling reassuringly.

We say our goodbyes to everyone and head back outside. I turn to walk toward our room, but Cooper pulls me in a different direction. We head over to some benches that are on the side of the building. He sits down and pulls me down next to him.

"What's going on, Cass?"

"Nothing. Why?" I try to sound flippant. He knows I am keeping something from him, but up until this point, he hasn't pushed.

"Don't give me that bullshit, Cass. I know you. I know you are keeping something from me, and I don't like it. We have to be open with each other. There are going to be times when we need to lean on each other. I can handle whatever it is." He pauses, looking down at the ground. His breathing has picked up and he won't look at me. "Are you... are you leaving me?"

"Oh my God, Cooper! No! Absolutely not! I can't believe you would even think that!" I say, crawling into his lap and making him look at me. "Coop, I love you. I will never, ever leave you. I'm so sorry that I made you even contemplate that."

He pulls me into a spine-crushing hug. "Thank God!"

"Coop. Coop, you're crushing me."

"Oh, sorry. My mind... I was just imagining the worst-case scenario, you know. And for me, that would be having to live my life without you." He leans his forehead against mine. "Cass, if something ever happened to you. If I ever lost you, I wouldn't be able to go on living. I just couldn't."

I just close my eyes. I can't look at him right now. I am being crushed from the inside with tremendous guilt and there is no way in the world I could ever tell him. But I also can't change my plans. I have to do this.

He pulls back and cups my face. "Then tell me what is going on in your head. I know something is up, Cass. I know you better than I know myself and something is bothering you."

"It's just... I..."

"Baby, whatever it is, we will get through it together," he says.

Unfortunately, no. We won't be getting through this one together.

Chapter 2
Realization

Cassidy

I managed to convince Cooper, somehow, that I was upset about the nightmares. I admitted that I had been having them for a while, which he was not happy about. But fortunately, he bought the whole thing. He thinks that that is what I have been keeping from him. How terrible am I? I am happy that my boyfriend bought my lie. Well, it's not really a lie. I have been having nightmares for a while, and I have been hiding them from him. It's just not the only thing I have been keeping from him.

We are sitting at dinner with Austin and the Chipmunks. They are laughing and razzing each other about things they have done over the years. They have all known each other since basic training so they have a lot of stories to tell. I am trying to laugh at all the appropriate places, but I keep getting lost in my head. Cooper keeps shooting worried glances at me and he hasn't taken his hand off my thigh yet.

"What's up your ass, Cass?" Austin asks, throwing a grape at me. Luckily for him, it missed, or I would have had to start a food fight. Not exactly fitting of a soldier.

"Nothing. What's up yours?"

"Nothing my ass. You're never this quiet. Coop, what's her deal?" Austin turns to Cooper.

Cooper squeezes my thigh. I don't think he will say anything, but I really don't know for sure. When he winks at me and smirks, I know my secret about my nightmares is safe.

"I gave her quite the pounding last night so she's probably pretty tired," he says, nudging my brother.

"Ugh! Gross! Dude, that's just not right," Austin whines. He punches Cooper in the arm, which turns into a little wrestling match at the table.

"Boys, boys. Come on now. This is not behavior expected from a Marine," I say.

They separate but keep punching each other in the leg under the table. After a few minutes of them both complaining about their legs, Austin calls me out. "Seriously, though, Cass. What's up?"

I look over at Cooper, pleading with my eyes for him to back me up here. But he doesn't.

"Just tell him, Cass."

I shoot Cooper a look telling him he is going to pay for that, and then turn to my brother.

"Um. It's nothing really. Just tired."

"Cass has been having nightmares for the past few months about her time with Anderson," Cooper says, telling one of my secrets.

I look at him and narrow my eyes. I'm pissed. I don't need this right now. Now Austin is going to be all over me about this and I know he won't just let it drop.

"Thanks, Coop. Nice to know that I can count on you when I need to," I say, standing angrily from the table. I grab my tray and turn to leave.

Cooper grabs my arm and stops me from leaving. "Stop, Cass. He only wants to help you."

I shrug him off and stomp away. I slam my tray onto the garbage can and storm out the door. I know Cooper was only trying to help, but the guilt is eating me alive. I could almost handle it when I was only lying to Cooper. Almost. But now that Austin is involved, I can't do it.

I get outside and find myself picking up my pace. Within a few steps, I am full-out running. I take off into the trees, following a path that has been worn into the dirt. A lot of the soldiers here like to run to let off some steam. There are several paved paths all over the base, and a few unpaved trails through the forest that have just been worn down over time. I haven't taken any before, but I know that they all end up leading back to base at some point.

Thanks to all the training that Austin and Cooper have put me through, I am able to run for a while without getting winded, so that's exactly what I do. I weave through the trees, following the path. I just let go. I listen to the rustling of the leaves, and the sounds of the wildlife scurrying around me. I just run. It's hard to turn your mind off when it's so loud, but I try. I need to not think for a while. It's all I've been doing, and it is exhausting.

I end up stopping towards the fence along the perimeter of the base. There are a few downed trees here and it is very secluded. I head over to one of the logs and plop down. I need a few minutes. I have no idea how far I've run, or what time it is, but I can tell that it is getting dark. I know I don't have much time before I need to head back. There aren't any lights out here, so I need to leave so I can find my way back.

How am I going to get through this? I hate lying. I hate it. It makes me feel so terrible inside. But to be lying to the two most important people in my life, I feel downright dirty. I start to doubt everything. Do I really have to do this? I mean, really. If I don't go, what will happen?

I contemplate that for about half a second. But I know exactly what will happen. It will take even longer to take down that facility if we are able to do it at all. Anderson could get away. If we try to take it at any random time, he may not be there, and that's the whole point of all of this. If we don't stop him, he will just continue somewhere else.

Ok. So, let's just say, for shits and giggles, that we are able to take down the facility even if I don't do this, but Anderson escapes. We have a lot of men undercover at many facilities. We should be able to find Anderson at another facility. Then we would just start the planning process again, which would probably delay everything for another few months at least. Right now, we aren't planning on doing anything for at least a few months. If we add more time to that, we are looking at close to another year before we could make another attempt at him. How many women could he torture and kill in that time? How many men? More than I even want to think about.

Well, shit. I really don't have a choice. I owe it to everyone involved to do this.

And let's not forget the little detail of Shelby, the young girl who helped me when Anderson had me the first time. I promised her I would get her out. It's already been several months since we escaped. Who knows what they are doing to her? Who knows when Anderson will start his research and torture on her? I can't let that happen.

I really *don't* have a choice, do I?

Now I just have to figure out how to act normal until this happens. I can't let Cooper or Austin think that there is anything wrong. I can't make them worry. I will just have to keep them believing that I am upset over the dreams. Which, again, isn't exactly a lie.

Then something occurs to me that changes everything. I don't have to act normal. Sure, I don't want to worry them. But I have been looking at this the wrong way. If I only have a few more months left to live, I have to enjoy every single second with them. There will be no acting involved. I have to make the next few months, my last few months, all about them.

I get up and start making my way back down the path. It takes me a while to get back to the Mess Hall and by the time I get back, it is dark out. There are still a few people milling around but I don't see Cooper. I head back to our room hoping he is there. I stand outside the door for a moment, collecting myself. I know once I open this door, everything has to be different. I have to be different. I can't let Cooper think that anything is wrong.

I turn the knob and open the door slowly. I see Cooper right away. He is sitting on the bed, leaning forward with his head in his hands. When he hears the door open, he glances up. Our eyes meet for just a brief second, and then he looks back down. It's at that moment that I realize just how badly I have been messing everything up. I acted like a complete brat at dinner. I had no right to yell at him and storm off.

I make my way over to him slowly and sit down. He doesn't acknowledge me at first, which worries me.

"I'm sorry," I say quietly.

Nothing. No response. His leg is shaking, which he only does when he is nervous about something. I've only seen him do it on a few occasions.

"Cooper, please. Look at me."

He takes a deep breath and slowly raises his head. When he finally meets my eyes, I am shocked. His eyes are wet with unshed tears. I immediately cup his face and pull him to me. I hug him with all that I have. He wraps his arms around me and squeezes. We sit there holding each other for a while, not saying anything. I can tell that he needs this. I have never seen him cry.

When he finally pulls back, he sighs. "Please, please tell me what's going on, Cass. I can't take this. I feel like I am losing you and you are right here."

I feel like shit. I debate for half a second on telling him the truth. But that thought leaves almost as quickly as it came. I can't. I have to protect him. I have to.

"I'm so sorry, Cooper. The nightmares are tearing me apart," I say, not lying. I have been struggling with them. I can deal with nightmares. I can. It's the fact that I can feel him kill me each and every time. The pain is real. "I wish I could explain it better. But the part that bothers me the most is the fact that the pain is real. I wake up each time in pain. I can *feel* the pain."

"Why didn't you tell me?" he asks, grabbing my hand.

"I didn't want to worry you. We have enough going on with the world going to shit, the last thing you need is to worry about me having stupid dreams. And on top of that, I don't want you worrying about me when you should be focusing on the missions. If something were to happen to you because you were distracted," I say, but am unable to finish that last thought.

He pulls me into his lap so that I am straddling his legs. He cups both sides of my face with his hands gently. "Cassidy, we are a team. If something affects you, it's my problem, too. Just like I would tell you if something was bothering me. I want you to come to me with these things so that I can bear part of the burden for you. That's what I am here for."

I just nod, not sure I am able to say anything at this moment.

"Cass, look at me. I am going to marry you at some point. When all this insanity is done, when we finally get to start our lives, that's the first thing that I'm going to do. I want to find a house on a nice piece of land where we can grow old together. I need you to trust me. I can handle a lot, Cass. Please don't shut me out again," he pleads.

I lean in and kiss him. "I'm so sorry, Coop."

"Don't be sorry. Be you." He pulls me into him and just holds me. I can hear his heart beating, feel each breath that he takes.

"Can I tell you about them?" I ask quietly into his chest.

He pulls back and looks right into my eyes. "Of course."

So, I do. I tell him about the torture. I tell him about being able to feel the pain, the agony. It takes a while, but I pour it all out. And throughout it all, Cooper is there, holding my hand. When I finish, he just pulls me down on top of him as heliess on the bed. He rubs his hands, up and down my back, soothing my pain.

I wish I could freeze this moment and live in it forever. I don't ever want to forget how it feels to be in his arms. My sanctuary. My home. I promise myself that no matter what happens, no matter what my future holds, I will remember this exact moment. I will remember this feeling forever.

Chapter 3
On Our Way
Cassidy

We spend the next day in the supply rooms, packing everything that we will need for the mission. This time is a bit different because we need to pack the tents and sleeping bags. We have to prepare for a night in the woods.

Austin and I used to sleep in the backyard of our parent's house, back before he left for basic training. We would set up a tent and pretend that we were on some big adventure. We alternated between hiking Mount Everest, to exploring the jungles of South America. We had so many good times in that tent. I wonder if Mom and Dad still have it... I stop for a minute. I almost forgot that they were gone. That we lost them both.

"What's wrong, kid? Did you see a spider?" Austin teases.

I look up at him and smile wanly. "Aus, do you remember how we used to camp in the backyard back home?"

He smiles. "Of course, I remember. Those are some of my favorite memories with you, kid." He comes over and pulls me into a hug. "You were thinking about them, weren't you?"

I just nod, a few tears falling down my cheeks.

"They would be so proud of you, Cassidy. So proud. You have become such an amazing woman. Beautiful, strong, smart. Well, and amazing. I know that they are watching us. I know it in my heart," Austin says, pulling back to look at me.

I wipe my tears. "Thanks, Austin. I think I really needed to hear that."

He pulls me into another hug, just as Cooper comes in. "Hey guys, do you think four bags of Doritos is enough for two days?" He must notice me crying and stops. "Hey now, what's this? Why the tears?"

Austin releases me and I go right into Cooper's arms. "Nothing. Just thinking about my mom and dad."

"I'm so sorry you lost them, baby. I really am. But you are not alone," Cooper tries to soothe me.

Time to buck up bronco. "I know, Coop. And to answer your question, yes. I think four bags of Doritos is more than enough."

"I don't know. We will be sleeping in tents in the woods. I will need the snackies," he says, rubbing his absolutely flat stomach.

We continue packing our supplies, and loading up the vehicles. Everyone who will be involved is here, getting their own supplies.

"Hey. I had an idea," Cooper says out of the blue.

"Oh, no," Austin says.

"No, no. I swear. It's a good one this time," he says.

I laugh at them. They are like two peas in a pod.

"Ok, Coop. What has your genius mind come up with now?" I ask.

"Right. So, I know we are taking this facility at night. And we are planning on using similar explosives as last time."

"Yes," I draw out.

"What if we were to set off some fireworks, you know, to draw them out?" he continues.

"Nope," Austin and I both say at the same time.

"No, listen. It could work. It would just take a little fire," he says seeming truly excited about the thought of using fire.

"No! There will already be explosives, we don't need any more fire you pyromaniac," I say laughing.

"You guys are no fun," he whines.

"Where would you even get fireworks, you idiot?" Austin asks.

"Oh, I have my ways," he says with an evil smile.

We finish packing, having spent the entire day here at the warehouse. We are all tired and hungry, but also anxious about this next mission. We leave in the morning, so we have to make sure we get a good night's sleep. We all head to dinner together. I am thankful that dinner is a simple meal of grilled chicken and vegetables. I don't think I could handle one of the chef's crazier meals tonight.

Cooper and I finish our meal and say goodnight to everyone, making our way back to our room. We don't speak on our walk, but he holds my hand the entire way. Once we get back, we both get changed and ready for bed. When we lay down, Cooper does what he always does and pulls me into him as he wraps his arms around me.

We lay there in silence for a while, so long, that I think Cooper has fallen asleep. I lazily run my fingers up and down the arm that he has wrapped around my waist.

"What are you thinking about?" he asks me quietly, alerting me to the fact that he is awake.

"Just thinking about how lucky I am that I found you," I say because I am.

"I'm the lucky one, Cass." He holds me for a while longer, absently drawing patterns on my skin. "It's ok, you know. You can go to sleep, and I'll protect you from the bad dreams. I will always protect you," he says, squeezing me tighter.

"I know, Coop. I know."

I guess that's exactly what I needed to hear because I find my eyes getting heavier. Just as I am about to go under, I hear "I will always protect you."

. . . .

The next morning is a whirlwind of activity as we all get ready to leave. We shove food in our mouths and rush around like chickens with our heads cut off as we get the last of the supplies into the vehicles. Austin, Cooper, and I are in the lead vehicle, with the

Chipmunks directly behind us, and the rest of the squad following in the last two trucks. Just as we are about the leave, Mike and Colonel Walters approach the group.

Everyone salutes, even me this time. "At ease. We came to send you off," Mike starts, looking around and making eye contact with all of his men. He stops when he gets to me. "I know that I don't have to remind you of the precious cargo that you carry. She is as much a part of this regiment as the rest of you, but she is also one of the viable females. Protect her with all that you are, men. Protect each other and come back stronger."

The men all shout their responses and soon we are on our way.

"I would suggest that we play the license plate game while we drive but since most of the roads are abandoned, so I guess that won't work," Cooper says.

"We could play twenty questions," I say.

"Or truth or dare," Austin says, wiggling his eyebrows.

I don't really want to play anything involving telling the truth right now, so I adamantly suggest twenty questions again. Unfortunately, I lose, and we end up in an annoying game of truth or dare.

"Cassidy," Cooper starts. "Truth or dare."

"Dare," I say immediately.

"I dare you to get on the radio and sing Baby Got Back," he says while laughing.

"Pshhh. I can do that," I say, grabbing the radio.

"Hold up, hold up," Austin says. "Let me get this party started right."

He grabs the radio from my hands and makes an announcement of sorts so that the guys in the other trucks know what is going on. "All right, gents. For your listening pleasure today, my sister, the amazing Cassidy, is about to entertain you all by singing Baby Got Back as part of her dare in our game of Truth or Dare," Austin says and hands me the radio.

Not one to shy away from a dare, I grab it and immediately start singing. "I like big butts and I cannot lie," I sing. I have to admit, my rendition is quite spectacular. When I finish, there is a resounding chorus of horns honking, lights flashing and screams through the radio. Austin and Cooper are laughing their asses off.

"Well, I don't think Sir Mix-a-Lot has anything to worry about with that performance," Austin teases.

"All right, Aus. If you're so confident. Truth or Dare?" I ask him.

"Truth," he says quickly.

I giggle to myself, thinking this is the best opportunity for me to get some long overdue information.

"Ok. What happened between you and Christie Nelson back in high school that made her hate you so much?"

"Uh. Dare, I choose dare," he says quickly, trying to change his selection.

"Nope. You can't change your mind after the question. You have to answer," I sing at him, poking him in the side.

"Ugh. I can't believe I have to tell my little sister about that night," he says, rolling his head back in defeat.

"Wait. Is this the girl that you left stranded out at the lake naked?" Cooper asks.

"What!" I scream.

Austin turns beet red and nods his head.

"Ok. You definitely have to explain now."

"It was a big misunderstanding. I went out to the lake with some of the guys. Christie and her friends were there drinking. She asked me to help her get something out of her car and I agreed. When we got to her car, she leaned in the back, to what I assume was to get said thing. Only she stood up without her top on. Her tits were just there. I had no interest in her, whatsoever, so I jumped in my truck and took off. So, she wasn't naked, per se. But I did leave her there topless."

I am laughing so hard I am afraid I am going to pee my pants. "Stop, stop. I can't believe you did that," I say, still laughing.

"Yeah, neither could she. She was so mad at me that she started telling everyone I was gay. Not exactly one of my prouder moments."

"Well, I can't imagine why," Cooper says.

"Ok, Coop. Truth or Dare?" Austin asks him.

Cooper thinks about it for a few minutes before he answers. "Truth and be nice. Remember that I am in love with your sister."

Austin just laughs maniacally.

"At what age did you lose your virginity?" Austin asks him.

There must be a story to this because Cooper shoots Austin a death glare. "You have to answer," Austin sings as I did to him.

"Fine. I was sixteen," Cooper says.

I just stare at him with wide eyes. "Wow, Coop. You weren't wasting any time, were you?"

"That's not the best part," Austin says.

"Wait. What's the best part?" I ask, extremely interested in his answer.

"He lost his virginity to his babysitter," Austin laughs.

"Wait, wait. You're making it sound like I needed a babysitter at the age of sixteen. It was the girl who used to babysit me when I was younger," he tries to explain as if that makes it sound any better.

"How old was she?" I ask, needing this information.

Cooper pauses, obviously not wanting to answer the question. "She was twenty-two."

I just about lose it at his admission. "That is the greatest thing I have ever heard," I say, laughing at the horrified look that Cooper has on his face right now.

"And just how did she like it, Coop?" Austin continues the line of questioning.

"She laughed at me," Coop admits sheepishly.

The rest of the trip continues along this path with me always selecting dare and completing the dares and the boys going back and forth outing all their embarrassing stories to me. It is the most fun I have had in my entire life, and I know that I will never forget this moment for as long as I live. No matter how long, or short, that is.

Chapter 4
Camping Cassidy

We finally get to our campsite around dusk. We are about sixty miles away, however many clicks that is in Military talk as the boys would say, and we are setting up camp. The woods are thick here, with not much room between each tree to set up our tents, but it is the best spot for us to stay hidden. Cooper sets up our tent, while I go over some of the equipment with Private Trottman, or Joe as I call him. As much as they have tried to drill the whole soldier thing into me, I still can't call them by their titles. Nope, just names for me, or nicknames.

We are sitting around a fire, eating our rations, ok so maybe I did pick up some of the lingo, and the boys are all telling more stories. It is funny to hear the Chipmunks talk about Cooper and Austin from back in their basic training days.

"And then Cooper comes around the corner, his pants around his ankles," Al is saying but has to stop talking because he is laughing so hard.

"But don't worry, he stopped to salute our Captain, balls out and everything," Teddy finishes for him.

Cooper just shakes his head. "You know, guys. You could tell some non-embarrassing stories of me. I mean, come on. Cassidy is sitting right here," Cooper complains. "And it's not my fault they called for me when I was taking a shit!"

Austin is laughing so hard he is rolling on the ground. I pat Cooper on the back. I am sitting on a log, and he is sitting between my legs on the ground, arms resting on my knees. "Don't worry, honey, I still love you."

"Awe, how sweet. Gag," Austin says as he gets himself back up on his log.

Cooper goes to punch him, but Austin ducks to avoid it, only knocking himself back off the log and onto the ground.

"All right, all right, you idiots. Let's keep it down. We are trying to stay hidden," one of the guys says.

"Why don't we go over the whole thing, one more time tonight, before we all turn in," Cooper says. "This is Cassidy's first-time running point on communications, and I want her to be ready."

I look down at Cooper. "Coop, I'll be fine. I promise. Joe will be with me the whole time."

"I know. But I want to know that you will be ok," he says, pulling me closer to him.

We go over the whole thing, step by step. It takes about an hour, with everyone listing their responsibilities. I have the timing down pat. I don't really have anything to do except to make sure that all the communications equipment is up and running properly. I have a laptop that I will have with me here where I can monitor the guys' locations and fix any equipment issues.

By the time they are done, I am exhausted. I am worried, as usual. Every time they go on one of these missions, I worry that I am going to lose one or both of them. Austin and Cooper are all that I have. I know that the rest of the men are technically my family, but it's not the same. Not even close.

Everyone says good night and we make our way to our tent. Cooper holds the flap open for me and I crawl in. It's not the roomiest tent, its main purpose is to be functional, not comfortable. We took our two sleeping bags and zipped them together like we did back in the cave, all those months ago.

"I know it's not the Hilton, but..." Cooper says shrugging.

"Hey. It's perfect. I was just thinking how this reminds me of the cave," I say.

He smiles. "Yeah. That was back when you hated me," he teases.

"I didn't *hate* you. I was so confused then. I had developed all these feelings for you but hadn't really spoken to you. It was... unsettling, to say the least."

Cooper comes over and pulls me into him. "You will never know how much I hated myself for making you go through that at the prison. I wish like hell I could have just held you."

"I know, Coop," I say, as I go over to my bag to pull out something to sleep in.

Cooper is doing the same when I see him get a smirk on his face suddenly. "You know. I have heard that when it's cold out, the best way to stay warm is skin-to-skin," he says, pulling his shirt off and looking at me. He winks.

"You're just trying to get me naked," I say, throwing my shirt at him, which is probably the wrong move being that I am now standing here without a shirt on.

He comes over to me and pulls me into him. "Doesn't look like I had to try too hard," he whispers.

"Coop," I say with a warning. "There are ten other men all within a few feet of us. I don't want anyone to hear."

He starts pouting, his bottom lip sticking out and everything. I laugh. "Besides. I need... want you to just hold me," I say, almost slipping and saying how much I need him to hold me right now.

He stops pouting and looks at me. "You never have to ask me to hold you, Cass. Never."

He changes into a pair of cotton pants while I finish pulling on my sleep shorts and shirt. He crawls into the sleeping bag and holds it open for me. I crawl in and lay down in the crook of his arm, resting my head on his chest. He pulls me as close as possible and zips us up.

We lay there, neither of us speaking. I am listening to the sounds of the woods. I can hear crickets chirping, an owl hooting. There are snaps and rustles as the wildlife comes back to life now that we are quiet. It's peaceful and humbling at the same time.

I'm lost in my head again, thinking about how much everything has changed. It's a more violent world now. Every man for himself. And that's just it. It's about every man because there aren't many women left at all. When you decrease the world's population of women by three-quarters, it changes the entire dynamic of the world. I almost forget sometimes how dangerous it is for me to be out in the world, away from our safe little community back at the base. I know that Cooper and Austin would never let anything happen to me, but still. Just to think about how many men are out there hunting people like me, it's... unsettling.

"Cass? You still awake?" Cooper asks.

"Yeah," I say, kissing his chest.

He doesn't say anything for a moment.

"I just want to let you know, that if something were to happen to me tomorrow," he starts, but I stop him by leaning up and pressing my lips to his. It's a hard kiss. I'm not trying to start anything. Its only purpose is to shut him up.

I pull back and look at him. "Don't you even say it. Just don't. Every time you are about to go on a mission you start this, and I am not going to listen to it anymore. You will come back to me. You have to. You promised."

He just nods and pulls me back into him. We lay there in each other's arms, and both drift off to sleep, worrying about the other.

We wake up the next morning and spend the day going over the plan and checking our equipment. By mid-afternoon, the Chipmunks take off to make sure that they have enough time to get everything set up as far as the explosives go. We are using the explosives as a diversion to distract for the guys going in on foot. This facility is a bit larger than any of the ones we have taken down so far. It scares me a bit, but I try not to think about it.

As it begins to get dark, the boys get ready to take off. Austin pulls me aside to give me a hug.

"Be careful, Cass. Take care of yourself and we'll see you later tonight," he says.

"You be careful, Aus. You'd better come back to me," I say. "And, if you don't mind, can you watch Cooper's back, too?"

"Don't worry, kid. I'll make sure he comes back to you, too," he says, ruffling my hair, just the way I hate.

As he is walking away, Cooper is coming towards me. They fist bump each other as they pass. Cooper pulls me right into his arms. I throw my arms around his waist and squeeze with everything that I have.

"Easy, Cass. I promise, everything will be fine," he says, trying to soothe me.

I don't know what it is this time, but I have a bad feeling. "Just promise me that you'll come back to me. Promise, Coop."

He pulls me back so that he can look at me. "I promise, Cass. There isn't anything on heaven or Earth that could take me away from you."

He leans down and kisses me. The moment our lips touch, I push for more. I have this terrible feeling that this will be the last time I get to kiss him. I know, dramatic. But there is just something nagging me in the back of my mind.

Our kiss turns passionate, but it's short, to my dismay. When Cooper pulls back, he just leans his forehead against mine.

"I love you, Cass. I love you, so much," he says quietly.

"I love you, more, Coop."

"We will pick this up when I get back," he says.

He backs away, never taking his eyes off me until the very last second. He turns and gathers the men. They have a quick little chat, and then they are off. They are taking two of the vehicles about fifty miles, then making the rest of the trek on foot. Right before he disappears into the truck, he winks at me and blows me a kiss.

I stare at where they disappeared for a while, not wanting to take my eyes off where they last were for some reason. Joe, er, Private Trottman, comes up behind me and clears his throat.

"Do you want to check the comms?" he asks.

I just nod and make my way over to the vehicle with all the equipment. We go over everything and do our preliminary check. It's time to check our connection to the men.

"Coop? Radio check," I say, waiting anxiously to hear his voice.

"Hey, there, beautiful. Radio check is good," he says, cheekily.

Then come the groans. Because we are all on the same channel, they all heard his response.

"Dude, come on. You wouldn't answer Trottman like that," Austin complains.

"Well, actually I would. I think Trottman is a very beautiful man," Cooper says.

Trottman grabs the radio. "Ok. Radio check complete. We're out."

There are a few more chuckles over the radio before it goes silent. This is the part that I hate the most. The waiting. I am not good at waiting. Just sitting here thinking about what they are walking into makes me sick. It is about thirty minutes until go time and I can't sit still.

"Cassidy, you have to calm down," Joe says.

I stop pacing and look at him. He's right. Me being a basket case isn't going to change anything. And that's one of the main things the boys tried to teach me, that a soldier remains calm in any situation.

Trottman tries to distract me by talking about anything and everything and before I know it, Cooper's voice is coming over the radio. I jump over in front of it and pick up my headset.

"Teams, check-in," he commands.

"We are a go," Austin is the first to reply.

"Go, here," I think that was Teddy.

"Go," Wilkins says from the final team.

"Ok. We are a go. Stay tight, watch each other's six. Let's go boys," Cooper says.

The first explosion can be heard through the radio. We are too far away to hear it through the woods. Just like always, there is a lot of shouting of commands and cursing that can be heard over the radio. I work my magic to clean it up, trying to hear everything more clearly.

More shouting, more commands. This part is so nerve-racking. I can't even imagine what they are going through.

"Clear," someone shouts.

"Coop, on your left," Austin, I think.

Me fiddling with the knobs some more, trying to clean up our feed. We are so engrossed in the feed, that I don't see them coming up behind us. I feel the gun being pressed into my back first. As I look to my right, I see Joe as someone hits him in the head from behind. He drops to the ground, unconscious.

"If I were you, I wouldn't move, little one," a gruff voice says.

"What do you want?" I ask, flicking the switch that allows my voice to be carried to the team in the facility.

"Cass! What's wrong?" Cooper asks, immediately concerned.

"Take the headset off, and turn around slowly," the voice says again, nudging the gun into my back even harder.

"I will do whatever you want, just don't hurt me," I try to sound meek. I don't want this guy, or whoever he is with to know that I can fight.

I turn slowly and my heart drops. There are five of them. I might be able to take down one man, but five? No freaking way. They are all extremely dirty looking like they haven't showered in weeks. The smell confirms that. I leave the headset on and can still hear what is going on at the prison.

"Cass. Talk to me," Cooper urges in my ear.

"Let's just talk, ok?" I ask the men, trying to come up with some way to describe these guys to Cooper. "What do the five of you want with me?"

"I said take the headset off!"

"Cass, give me something. Just shout whatever you can, and I'll be there as soon as I can. Hold on, baby," Coop says, and that's the last thing I hear before I take it off. I don't pull it completely off my head. I drop it so that it is around my neck, the microphone sticking out in front of me.

"Ok. It's off. Now, let's talk about this," I say, trying to stay calm. I glance to my right and see that Trottman is still unconscious on the ground. "Why did you knock my friend out?"

"Well, hmmm. Let me think. Oh, yeah. It's because you are a chick, and I need some money. There are some people looking for girls and I can make a pretty payday by taking you in," Stinky says.

"I have money," I say, trying to think on the fly. "I can pay you whatever you want. I can even get you food and shelter. We can work something out."

He just laughs, and then his goons start laughing. They sound like a pack of hyenas.

"Honey, with the money I can get from you, I can buy all the food and supplies I will need for the rest of my life," he growls.

"You look familiar," I say, trying to grasp at straws. "Do I know you from somewhere? What's your name?"

"The name's Crawford and honey, you would know if we had met before. I wouldn't have let you forget any time we spent together," he says as he looks me up and down. I think I actually throw up in my mouth a little.

"Gross," I say.

The group of them start closing in on me.

"Where are you going to take me?" I ask, trying to think of anything to stall.

"See, there are rumors of this doc in D.C. that will pay the big bucks for any viable females. And sweetheart, you look extremely viable to me," he says, grabbing me.

I knee him in the balls quickly, which drops him to his knees.

"Well, *you* see, scumbag. I am not going to go quietly," I say, swinging out at the next asshole who tries to grab me. I manage to grab the gun at my waist and drop two of the goons before Stinky manages to slam a rock into my head from behind.

The last thing I hear before I lose consciousness is Cooper screaming into the radio.

"Cassidy!"

Chapter 6
Taken

Cooper

"Nooooo!" I scream.

The boys have just secured the last of the men fighting us, no thanks to me. As soon as Cassidy alerted me that there were people there with her, I stopped fighting and found a quiet corner where I could listen to everything. I could tell they told her to take the headset that she was wearing off because her voice was farther away. But I could still hear everything.

There were five of them. Well, at least there were five of them before she drew her weapon. That's my girl. Only, they still got her. At least she managed to take a couple down on her way out. But I heard the hit to her head. It sounded brutal. And now, I am beside myself with rage.

I get up and start running towards Austin. "Austin!" I shout, trying to get his attention. He is across the room. He probably heard what happened.

"Coop. What happened to Cassidy? I heard her talking, but couldn't make out what she was saying," he says, sounding almost as frantic as me.

"They took her," I say.

"Who took her? Where is she?" he asks quickly.

"There were five of them. She managed to take down two of them but the last I heard, they must have hit her in the head because she's gone," I say. "We have to go. Let the guys finish this up. We have to get back there. Maybe one of the guys she shot is still alive and we can question him."

He nods. We take off towards Wilkins. "Wilkins," I shout. "You're in charge. Aus and I have to head back. Cassidy was attacked," I say quickly.

"Fuck! Ok, no problem. We'll be back soon. Don't do anything crazy without us," he shouts.

Austin and I take off running. We make it back to the vehicles in half the time because we are both sprinting. We jump into one of the trucks and Austin speeds back through the woods.

"Aus, what if," I start, but can't finish. I don't even want to think about her being killed.

"Don't Coop. She's fine. She's tough. I'm sure she put up quite the fight. She'll be ok. I promise," he says.

We make the rest of the drive, in silence. Neither of us is willing to talk about what I know we both are thinking. That if they took her, they would hand her over to Anderson and his facility. They are offering the most money for females.

When we get back, my hopes are quickly dashed as there is no sign of Cassidy anywhere. I run right over to Trottman, who is leaning against one of the wheels of their communication vehicle.

"Trottman! What happened?" I ask.

He looks dazed, his eyes unfocused. "They snuck up on us," he says, rubbing his head. "We were so focused on the action and what you guys were saying that we didn't see them coming. They got me on the back of the head, and I went down, hard. I was in and out. I only caught a few of the things that they said. I know that she took those two down, but then she was laying on the ground next to me, bleeding from the head. They must have hit her hard."

I swallow, hard. "Did they say anything about where they were taking her?"

"Yeah," he says. "And you're not going to like it."

"D.C. They took her to Anderson, didn't they?" I say, not really needing him to confirm it.

He just nods.

Fuck! I kick the ground. I am screaming and throwing anything and everything I can get my hands on. Austin tackles me to the ground.

"Fuck!" I scream, as I finally start to calm down.

"You have to calm down, Cooper," Austin says in my ear. We are laying on the ground now, he has his arms wrapped around me from behind.

"I'm good," I snap. "I'm good! Let me up."

Austin stands up, but I just roll over and lay on my back.

"We have to get her back, Aus. I can't let her go through that again. I *promised* her I wouldn't let them take her again," I say, my heart pounding. How could I let this happen?

"We'll get her back, Coop. I swear it. But we have to gather the guys and get back to base. We have to have our heads about this. We have to make a plan. We can't just go in, guns blazing on this one. It has to be thought out," Austin says.

I get up and go over to the two guys that Cassidy shot. She got the first one right between the eyes, so he's dead. The second though, she got in the belly, and unfortunately for him, he's still alive. I kick him in the ribs, waking him up.

He is groaning like a little baby.

"Where are they?" I shout at him, kicking him again.

"I don't know. I don't know anything," he groans, grabbing his stomach.

He's not bleeding a lot, so it doesn't look like she hit anything vital. I lean over him and grab his shirt. I pull him up, so he is face-to-face with me.

"I will kill you if you don't tell me. And when I say kill, I mean kill you slowly and painfully, if you don't tell me where they took her."

"Ok! Ok! They went to some big place in D.C. Some doc named Anderson is paying big time for chicks. But only if they are alive. So, they didn't kill her. They wouldn't have. She's safe with them," he says, trying to reason with me.

Just as he finishes, the other vehicle pulls through the trees. Our men jump out and come running over.

"Where's Cassidy?"

"Is she ok?"

They all rattle off questions as fast as they can get them out. Austin comes up, thankfully, and fills them in on what happened. By the time he is done, I have reached my breaking point. I hear them talking about what happened after we left the prison.

"Let's go! We have to get back now!" I shout.

Austin comes over to me and puts his hands up to calm me down.

"Look. Here's the plan," Austin says, taking charge for me. "Cooper and I will take Trottman and head back to base. Wilkins will take the rest of the vehicles back to the prison and finish up there."

I just nod, making my way over to the truck. I help Trottman up and get him into the back, laying down with an icepack on his head. Once I have him set, I turn back to Austin. He claps me on the back and gets in the driver's side, knowing full well I am in no shape to drive right now.

Once we are on the road, and I have calmed down a bit, I turn to him.

"Aus, what are we going to do? I have to get her back. I have to. I can't live without her," I say, putting my head in my hands.

"Coop, I need her just as much as you do. We will get her back. We just have to get back up. We can't go in there alone. We would just get her and both of us killed."

I just nod. This is all my fault. I should have never left her alone there. I know Trottman was with her, but that's not nearly enough. This is all my fault.

When I come to, it's with a massive headache. That fucker hit me in the head and knocked me out. I take stock of the rest of my body, having a little bit of déja vu right now. My arms and legs are secured to a table. Unfortunately, I am in a room that I recognize, and I immediately start to panic.

I'm back. I'm back at the prison in Anderson's room. I have to calm myself down. If I am going to get through this, I need to calm down. I take some deep breaths, trying to slow my breathing and my heart rate. If he comes in and sees me like this, it will all be over. I can't let him know that he is already in my head. I have no idea how long I have been here or even what day it is. The last thing I remember is shooting those two idiots who were trying to hurt me.

Cooper.

The only hope that I have is that Cooper heard where they were taking me. He will come for me. I know it.

I'm sure that they know I am awake by now. I know there are cameras in here somewhere. He likes to record his torture. I picture him pleasuring himself watching the torture later. He is one sick fucker, that's for sure. I lift my head and check the rest of my body. I am dirty, but at least my clothes are still on this time. The last time I woke up like this, I was naked. My pants are all torn up, as if I was dragged through the woods. My shoes are gone, and my hands are all bloody, but other than that, everything seems ok. The only thing that hurts is my head. I try to bring my hand up to check, but I can't move my arms very much. I look around and take stock of the room but just like last time, the only thing in here is the table. The white walls and floor are bare. No chairs, no windows. Nothing. It's completely barren. There is nothing in here to use as a weapon. No chance of me getting free either. The ties that are holding me to the bed are the ones that you see in psychiatric hospitals, or at least the ones I remember from TV shows back in the day of watching television. Wow, that seems like so long ago.

I laugh a little. How life has changed.

I have spent the last few months feeling guilty for keeping my mission secret from Cooper and I ended up here anyway, without lying to him. Karma is a true bitch.

I hear the door open and look towards it.

And there he is.

"Honey, I'm home," I sing, smiling at Anderson, trying to hide the fact that I am freaking out on the inside.

"Oh, Miss Daniels. How I have missed you," he says while smiling. "I'm so glad your spirits are up, because I intend to knock them down a peg or two."

"Why not just go ahead and kill me? Why drag it out, you sick psychopath?" I taunt him. I don't know what it is about this man, but he really brings out the smartass in me.

"Oh, Miss Daniels. I am not going to kill you. I am going to break you," he says sardonically. I pause. Those are the exact same words he used in my dream.

"You can't break what's already been broken, asshole," I reply.

"But I can try," he says. "Just give in, Miss Daniels. You know I will win."

"And you know I will fight," I growl.

He glares at me for a moment before he leaves and slams the door. A second later, I hear the lock engage. He is toying with me already. Leaving me to think and worry about what he has in store for me. He is just about the mind games as much as he is the physical torture.

I have no idea how long I lay there, lost in my head before I hear the door opening again.

"Back so soon?" I smart off immediately.

"Cassidy?" a small voice says.

I look to my right at the sound of that voice and stop. It's Shelby.

"Shelby!" I exclaim, trying to get up to hug her, forgetting that I am tied down for a minute. "Oh, God! Shelby. Are you ok? Have they hurt you?"

She comes over to the bed and begins to untie me. I wonder why she is doing this. But that's when I notice Anderson's goons standing by the door. She's allowed to untie me because she has backup.

"I'm so sorry that you are back, Cassidy," she cries, throwing her arms around me once I am untied.

It's then that I really look at her. She has circles under her dark eyes like she hasn't been sleeping. Her dark brown hair is a mess, like it hasn't been washed in a while. She is thin, almost emaciated. We haven't seen each other in over six months but she looks so much older, almost like she has aged years.

"Oh, Shelby. What have they done to you?" I ask, pulling her close.

"I thought I would never see you again," she says.

"I told you I would come for you, didn't I? I know this isn't exactly what I meant, but I'm here now. I'll take care of you," I say. "Now tell me what's been happening with you."

She sits on the bed next to me. She doesn't speak immediately, only glancing up nervously at the two goons in the doorway.

"Give us some privacy you asshats. It's not like we can go anywhere," I say angrily.

They glance back and forth between each other, shrug, and then finally turn and leave. They close the door behind them and lock the door.

I turn back to Shelby and pull her into my arms again. She cries for a long time. I just hold her. It's all I can do right now. After a while, she seems to calm herself down and pulls back to look at me.

"What's going on, Shelby? Talk to me."

She sniffles and wipes her eyes. "Oh, Cassidy. It's been horrible. Anderson blamed me for you escaping. He thought that I had something to do with it. I pleaded with him. I begged. I swore to him that I had nothing to do with it. But he just took it out on me."

I gasp. I knew Anderson was sick, but to take something like that out on an innocent girl. This is all my fault. I never once stopped to think of her when Cooper and I were running. I am terrible. I am an awful human being.

"I'm so sorry, Shelby. This is all my fault. I can't believe Anderson would do this to you. You're just an innocent girl. How sick do you have to be to torture a sixteen-year-old girl?"

"I'm eighteen, Cassidy. I turned eighteen a few months ago," she cuts me off, correcting my misassumption.

"Oh! I totally thought you were younger."

"It's ok. I get it all the time. I have a young face," she says, wiping away a few more tears.

Then it hits me, suddenly. "Shelby, please tell me they didn't auction you off. Please, please, please tell me they didn't send you out there with those monsters," I say quietly.

She looks down at the floor, not answering me right away.

"No. I haven't been sent out there yet. He has been using me for research. I think he needs something. They have taken an awful lot of blood from me recently."

"Oh, Shelby. I can't tell you how sorry I am. I should have come back for you sooner. We've been making plans, taking down other facilities," I say, but stop short, realizing that they are probably listening to me.

Shelby shakes her head quickly, looking around the room. "Not here," she whispers.

I nod my head telling her that I understand.

We sit there together for a while, talking about what has been going on. I try to be as cryptic as possible while we whisper back and forth. She tells me about the testing that Anderson has been doing.

"He brings you up a lot. Not always directly to me, but almost like he is mumbling to himself. I hear him say things like 'that damn Daniels girl' and 'I'll get her back somehow.' I don't know why he is so obsessed with you. It's kind of creepy," Shelby says quietly.

I have wondered that as well. "I have no idea. It's probably my charm, that's why he must want me," I say, and we giggle about that together.

"Well, well, well. What do we have here? Getting chummy?" Anderson says. I hadn't even heard them open the door, which is very bad. If I have any chance of surviving this, I have to be on my toes at all times.

"Oh, good. I'm glad you're here, dickhead. We were just discussing how hungry we are. We will both take a cheeseburger, some fries and oh, I don't know. Shelby, do you want a chocolate shake or vanilla?" I ask, laughing as Anderson scowls at me.

Smack! The hit comes before I even see it coming. He backhanded me across the face. That one is going to leave a mark, for sure.

"So, that's a no on the food?" I ask, not being able to resist smarting off to him.

"You, Miss Daniels, have ten minutes to get yourself cleaned up. Girl! Take her to the shower. Quickly!" Anderson shouts at Shelby, making a move toward her.

Oh, hell no! He is not hitting her. I jump up and pull her behind me. "Don't touch her!" I warn him. He may have his goons here to protect him, but I am sure that I could get a few good hits in before they get to me.

He looks at me and grins. "Watch yourself, Miss Daniels."

He turns and stomps out of the room, leaving Shelby and me alone with the two goons.

"Let's go, bitch," goon number one says in a deep, menacing voice.

"We're coming," I say back to him, mocking him in a deep voice.

He stops walking and comes back over to stand in front of me. He is a good foot taller than me, the top of my head just reaching his chest. He grabs a fist full of my hair on the back of my head and cranks my head backward. It happens so quickly, my neck cracks, and it doesn't tickle.

"The same rules don't apply this time, girl. Last time you were here, we weren't allowed to touch you. This time... well, let's just say I would sleep with one eye open if I were you," he says, throwing me to the ground. "That, is your only warning, bitch."

Shelby rushes over to me and helps me up. The goons are waiting for us in the doorway. I may like to be a smartass, but something about his warning has me shutting my mouth. Why is this time different? What exactly does he have in store for me? And most importantly, can I survive?

Chapter 8
Let It Begin
Cassidy

Shelby took me to the showers and left me alone for a bit. I take my time in the shower because part of me knows that this is the last alone time I will get for a long time, if at all. I stand here, under the water, thinking about Cooper and what he must be going through right now. He was on the radio when everything happened. I don't know how much he heard, or if he was able to tell what was going on, but I know that he knows what happened. Whether or not he picked up on where they were taking me is unknown. But if I know Cooper, the first place he will look is here. He knows what Anderson did to me. He knows what he wanted from me but didn't get. He wanted me pregnant so that he could do more experiments on me. But I guess that didn't work out for him, did it?

I wish I knew what Anderson's problem is with me. I don't get it. I was only here for about nine days. Sure, we had our joyful time together – I'm being sarcastic, just in case you couldn't tell. But aside from that, I did nothing to him personally. I survived his torture. Maybe that's it. Maybe it's just the fact that he didn't get to kill me. I know I am a smartass and I made it my goal to get under his skin, but that can't be the real reason he is obsessed with me.

I really wish Cooper was here with me. I miss him, so badly, already. It's been less than twenty-four hours, at least I think that's all it's been. I wrap my arms around myself, trying to create the feeling he gives me when he is holding me, but it's not the same. Nothing could ever feel as good as it does when his arms are around me.

I am stalling, I know it. But I am not looking forward to whatever he is going to do to me. I know that he will make it hurt. I can just picture the sadistic smile he gets on his face when I am in pain. I can only imagine how bad it is going to be. I try to prepare myself by doing some of the deep breathing that Austin taught me when he was teaching me to keep calm in every situation. I don't think anything I do right now will prepare me for what's ahead. It will be brutal. But that's not the part that gets me. The part that kills me, no pun intended, is that he is going to kill me. I know that. How do you prepare yourself to die? How do you get ready for pain? The answer – you can't. I didn't get to say goodbye to Cooper or my brother. I didn't get to tell them that I love them and that I am doing this for them. The only thing that makes this even slightly bearable is the thought that they will take down this facility in the end.

I turn off the water and make my way over to the pile of clothing that Shelby left for me. She was crying when she left. I tried to assure her that I would be ok, but she just kept apologizing, as if any of this is her fault. I pull the stupid slip dress on over my head and finger-comb my hair. What does someone have to do to get a brush around here? I knock on the door to let them know that I am done. The door opens after a second, and I gasp but quickly recover.

Jax is standing there with a frown on his face. He subtly shakes his head, letting me know that I have to pretend that I don't know him. I change my face to a scowl and take a step back.

"Let's go, girl," he says, harshly, but I can tell by the look on his face that he is anything but mad. He looks upset.

Trying to keep up appearances and all, I smart off to him. "Oh, how sweet. You're quite the charmer with the ladies, aren't you?"

He backhands me across the face and my head whips to the side. I catch myself before I fall and turn to shoot him a look. He looks apologetic. I know what he is silently saying.

I get up and walk over to him so he can slip the ties onto my wrists. Once they are secure, he drags me out of the room and down the hall. I take in my surroundings again. There are quite a few more people milling around this time. Not just guards, either. I see some medical staff, all wearing white lab coats, and what look like janitors, pushing little carts of cleaning equipment. What is going on? Someone walks by pushing an incubator. They have babies here?

When we get back to what I am now calling "my room," Anderson is standing there waiting.

"Get her strapped down," he says to Jax. "I'll be back in a few minutes to get started."

"Yes, sir," Jax agrees.

He takes me into the room and closes the door behind him. As soon as we are alone, he lifts his hand and pushes a button on some fancy-looking watch that he is wearing.

"There. I only have a few minutes before they come in to see what is going on. I just sent an impulse to knock out the cameras and sound temporarily," he says, but I don't give him a chance to finish. I knee him in the balls, and he drops to the ground.

"That, is for slapping me, you ass," I say, helping him back up.

He chuckles. "Yeah. I deserved that. Sorry, Cass. But I had to keep up appearances," he says.

"I know, I know. Quick, tell me what's going on."

"Ok. Here's what I know. Anderson thinks he is on to something, but he needs to do some more research to test his theory. It has something to do with the women who seem to be immune, meaning you, and what he thinks is the key to protecting the rest of the women. I have no idea what that means for you," he says, rubbing his crotch. "Jeez, Cassidy. Why did you have to go for the jewels? You got them both!"

"Why are there so many more people around now?" I ask, ignoring his complaints.

"It has something to do with you being here, but I don't know for sure."

"What is his problem with me, anyway? Why is he so focused on me?"

"The only thing I can think of is that he lost his daughter in the first wave. Maybe you look like her or something," he says, guiding me over to the gurney that he has to strap me to.

"Have you talked to Cooper?" I ask solemnly.

He just shakes his head. "I'm supposed to check in with them shortly. What do you want me to tell him?"

I sigh. I know what I want to say. I want to tell him to get me out of here. I want to say that I love him, and I need him. But I don't. "Tell him not to come yet. Tell him that I am ok, but I need some time to figure out what is going on. And tell him..." I pause, choking back a sob. "Tell him that I love him, but I have to stay here and get some information."

Jax stops what he is doing and looks at me sadly. "Cassidy," he starts, but I stop him.

"Don't Jax. I have to do this. I was going to be coming here anyway, it just happened faster than I expected."

He looks confused, but nods. We are running out of time. He tells me that he will find a way to talk to me again soon and that I should wait for him to come to me. He doesn't want me doing anything that may expose him. They don't suspect him at this point and that is what we need.

Just as he finished attaching the ties to my legs the door opens, and Anderson walks in, pushing a tray of syringes. A man follows behind him with some type of machine.

"Leave," he barks at Jax, who just nods and leaves without a glance back at me. I know he can't let on that he knows me, but it still hurts. Would it have killed him to wish me good luck, or I don't know, maybe a 'don't die' would have been nice.

"Okey, dokey, prick. Whatcha got in your little arsenal this time?" I ask, trying to piss him off right away.

He laughs. "Oh, Miss Daniels. We are going to have so much fun this time. First things first, though. I need some blood and other samples," he says, snapping on a pair of gloves. How cliché. He looks like the quintessential mad scientist right now.

The other man that came in the room with him, comes over and jams a needle into my arm. I grunt but just cooperate, for now. He takes several vials of blood and then pulls the needle out. He doesn't even try to stop me from bleeding, which to be perfectly honest, pisses me off a bit. My blood is slowly dripping onto the floor.

Unfortunately for me, the table that I am strapped to puts me in the perfect position for them to do all kinds of things. My arms are tied out to the sides, and my legs are tied to two separate parts of the table. Anderson comes over and pulls a lever on the table that allows him to separate my legs. Since I am wearing a dress, this does not allow me much modesty.

"What? You're not even going to buy me dinner first?" I say as he moves between my legs. I know what is coming. It is what they did last time. They are checking my lady bits.

Anderson sneers at me with my comment and proceeds to flip my dress up so that my bottom half is completely exposed. I am completely embarrassed and terrified of what he is going to do, but I can't let him see that. He jams his fingers into me and pauses. He has a deep frown on his face as he looks back up into my eyes. "Well, well, Miss Daniels. It seems you have been busy since you were last here. Not a virgin anymore. Quite the little slut."

I balk at him, utterly speechless, which doesn't happen to me often.

He proceeds with his... exam and sticks all kinds of things in me that hurt. I have been to the gynecologist before, so I recognize some of the things, and there are swabs and vials in addition to the blood they took. I have no idea what he will do with all my samples, and honestly, I don't want to know. But unfortunately, I have to find out.

"So, doc. What exactly are you testing me for this time? Or are you just upset that I cheated on you? That's it, isn't it? You wanted me all for yourself," I taunt him.

"You know, Miss Daniels. Most people would lay still and be quiet when they are in such a predicament. But not you. No. You, my dear love to get under my skin," he says, pulling his gloves off. He turns and hands the tray of samples to the other man, who I am now calling Skinny Joe in my head. He looks like a real tool. Tall, skinny, glasses, perfectly coifed hair. It's disgusting.

"Get the tests started. I want to know as soon as you have results so I can continue," Anderson snaps at him. He just nods, grabs the tray, and leaves the room, leaving Anderson and I alone.

"So, seriously. What is it with you? Why the obsession with me? Is it because I look like your dead daughter or something?"

Wrong thing to say.

He grabs a syringe off the table and jams it into my arm angrily. He doesn't hesitate to push on the plunger, injecting a nasty-looking blue liquid into me. I immediately scream and beg him to stop. So much for not letting him see me cry. I scream and thrash around, trying to free myself. I need to curl up into a little ball, then it won't hurt so much. At least that is what I am telling myself. The fire burns inside of me, just like last time. I am in so much pain, I almost miss what he says to me.

"If you ever bring up my daughter again, I will kill you, Miss Daniels. And it won't happen quickly," he growls at me and then leaves me to scream in agony.

Chapter 9
So Much Anger
Cooper

"Someone needs to tell me something right fucking now before I lose it," I scream. We are in the planning room in the Administration building back at the base. We've been back for about twelve hours, and I know no more now than I did twelve hours ago.

Austin comes up to me and tries to calm me down. "Chill, man. I'm upset, too. But we have to keep our heads if we are going to get her back." He always was the calmer one between the two of us.

We have been in this room, waiting on the General for about thirty minutes, but it feels like days. All I can think about is what they are doing to her, right now. My chest hurts. It's almost like I can feel the pain that I know she is in. I pace back and forth across the room, running my hands through my hair as if that is going to bring her back to me.

"Fuck!" I scream to no one in particular.

"Take it easy, Staff Sergeant Matthews," General McConnell says as he makes his way into the room. I immediately stand at attention, saluting my superior. I may be pissed beyond belief, but I am still a U.S. Marine through and through.

"At ease, son. Come have a seat and let's talk about what we know," he says, motioning for Austin and me to take a seat near him.

I sit down, but I can't sit still. My leg is shaking, something I do when I am nervous. Austin fills him in on what happened when they took Cassidy. He tells him about what I heard on the radio, knowing full well that I am in no condition to give a report at this point. His sister is missing. My Cassidy is missing! How could he be so calm?

"Ok. So, we have her on the inside now. Maybe we will get some good intel now," he says.

Wait, what? I'm so angry that it sounded like he said he was glad she is there right now.

"Excuse me, sir. But what the fuck?" I say, jumping up from my chair. Austin tries to pull me back down, but I pull my arm out of his grasp. "Every second that she is gone, is another second that she is being tortured and beaten. How can you actually think that we should leave her there just to get information?" I am shouting, and this is not behavior becoming a U.S. Marine, but I just can't find it in myself to care right now.

Austin jumps up to apologize for me. "I'm sorry, sir. It's just that we are both extremely worried about Cassidy right now and our main focus is getting her back."

"I get it gentlemen. I really do. But this was the plan all along," he says, completely baffling me.

Austin and I just stare at him. "Sit down, boys, so I can explain." We both fall numbly back into our seats and just stare at him. What, in the actual fuck, does he mean?

"Beg your pardon, sir, but... what do you mean this was the plan all along?" I ask.

He sighs and rubs the bridge of his nose like he is exhausted. I really look at him then and notice the bags beneath his eyes, the way he looks like he has aged ten years overnight.

"I wasn't supposed to have to tell you this yet. She didn't want you two to know," he starts. "The Colonel and I approached Cassidy about six months ago with a secret mission. We asked her to go back into Dr. Anderson's facility to get us information on what he is researching. Jax has been invaluable to us with the information that he has been able to provide, but we need someone who can get close to Anderson himself. That is the only way we can get what we need to bring him down. Cassidy took a long time to think about it. And I have to tell you, that the decision was not easy for her. She knew that she would be leaving the two of you behind and that you would be extremely angry with her. She finally agreed with the stipulation that you two only be notified if absolutely necessary. Now, what happened last night was not part of the plan, but it put us right where we need to be right now. Jax has already been in contact, letting us know that she is there and that he is keeping an eye on her. She will get information to him and he to us. Once we have everything that we need, we will go and get her out. The plan is to take down the facility and capture Anderson."

I jump to my feet and slam my fists down onto his desk. "There is no way that Cassidy would keep this from me. No way! And who do you think you are asking her to do this?"

The General jumps to his feet and yells right back. "I am a General in the United States Army and I have every right to ask this of anyone! It is my responsibility to put an end to this madness, this chaos that Anderson and the government have caused. I have to do everything in my power to stop it! Do you think it comes easy to me to put someone as sweet and innocent as Cassidy in danger? Do you think I really want her to get hurt?" He pauses, allowing us to consider what he is saying. He sighs heavily and sits back down. "I have spent my career sending men and women to their deaths, all by giving a simple order. It haunts me each and every day the number of good men and women, good soldiers that have died because of my orders. The last thing that I want is for Cassidy to be killed."

I just look him dead in the eyes and say what needs to be said. "I get it, General. I do. But you are forgetting one simple thing. The most important thing. Cassidy... is not a soldier."

"You are correct, Cooper, she is not a soldier. But we are in a war that is being fought by anyone who is willing and able. She knew what was being asked of her," he starts, and I cut him off.

"You have asked her to die!"

"No! I have asked her to do anything and everything to help us end this war. We will get her out when the time is right. But I am ordering you not to do anything until we are ready. We need to plan. We need to be ready when we go into that facility. If we do it wrong, she will get killed. If we rush, she will die. This must happen in the right order, or she. Will. Die," the General says, his anger with me obvious.

He's right. I know it. I fall, defeated, back into my chair.

"We'll get her back, Coop. I'll die before I let that fucker kill her," Austin says, trying to reassure me.

"I'm sorry. I truly am, gentlemen. But I promise you that I will exhaust every measure, every resource, to get her out alive. But we have to look at the big picture here. Taking him down is our biggest priority. We have to stop him. The fate of so many women depends on it," the General says as if that makes me feel any better.

I lean forward and put my head in my hands. What I wouldn't give to charge into that facility right now and kill him. The thoughts that are running through my head right now are dangerous. I know that she is in pain. I can feel it.

But, if it's the last thing I do, I will kill him. And God help anyone who gets in my way.

Chapter 10
The Biggest Shock of My Life
Cassidy

I wake to the sound of beeping. Everything hurts. Everything. I'm not quite ready to open my eyes yet, though. It hurts too much. I lay there, thinking about my situation. What I have gotten myself into. This is not going to end well, that much I know. So, at least I know that part of this has to do with Anderson's dead daughter. The way he reacted proves it. But what exactly about her? I wonder if he tried to save her and failed. I know how hard it is to lose family. I really do. And part of me, an extremely small part, sympathizes with him. I lost both of my parents. One to this thing, and one to the aftermath. But that doesn't give him the right to do all of the things that he is doing.

I'm lost in my head for a while, not paying much attention when the door opens. My eyes shoot open, and I groan from the pain. My head is throbbing. I look over at the door and see Skinny Joe. He has what looks like a heart monitor with him.

"Ah, so you're finally awake," he comments.

"Yup. Sorry, but it's going to take a bit more than that to kill me."

He just shakes his head and makes his way over to me. He spends the next few minutes hooking me up to the machine. He puts stickers all over me – my chest, my legs, and my stomach. I can't imagine why they would be putting the probes on my stomach.

He finishes attaching everything and turns on the machine. I notice that the machine has two screens. The larger one immediately starts beeping with my heart rate. The smaller one is silent, with just a flat line going across the screen. He messes with the probes on my stomach, moving them around until a faster beeping sound is heard.

I gasp. No. It can't be.

"Ah. There's the little tyke," Skinny Joe says, smiling.

"Th... the... the little tyke?" I manage to get out.

"So, you didn't know then," he says. "You're pregnant, Miss Daniels. About seven weeks from my calculations. I guess I should congratulate you. Or... offer my condolences. This is going to make things quite a bit, uh, let's just say, unpleasant for you."

I'm pregnant. I'm pregnant. I feel a tear running down the side of my face. I immediately panic. I don't care if he kills me, but my baby. My baby! Cooper's baby! I can't allow that to happen. This changes everything.

"You have to tell him! You have to tell Anderson not to do anything," I beg in an absolute panic.

He just laughs. "Oh, my dear. This is exactly what we were hoping for," he says as he makes his way out of the room.

I cry. I cry for my baby. I cry for Cooper. I cry for the life that we could have had if I wouldn't have been taken. A baby.

He said that this is exactly what they were hoping for? Meaning he wants to experiment on me while I am pregnant? Why? Why would anyone want to hurt an unborn child? How sick do you have to be? I have to get out of here. I have to. I can't let him kill my baby.

I lay there for what feels like an eternity, just watching the little heartbeat. I am mesmerized by it. This little baby, this little bean of life, is the product of my love for Cooper, and his love for me. And I can do nothing to protect it. I wonder if it is a boy who will look like Cooper, or a little girl, who looks like me. I wonder what it would feel like, to hold my little baby. Cooper is going to make the most amazing father. Or, at least, I hope he gets the chance to be one. I can't even imagine what will happen if he finds out. Will he be happy? We talked about having kids, once all of this was over. We both want a family. We just didn't expect that it would happen at this most inopportune time.

I must fall back asleep again because I am jolted awake by someone jamming something into my arm. Skinny Joe is back, and Anderson is standing over in the corner, messing around with something on a tray. Skinny Joe is putting an IV catheter in my arm and securing it with tape. There is already one in my other arm. I must have slept through him putting in that one.

"Rise and shine, sleeping beauty," Anderson says walking over to me. "I heard that you had no idea that you are pregnant. How wonderful that I get to be the one to break the news to you."

I shake my head. "No, I didn't. But this changes everything, Anderson. You can't hurt my baby. I'll do anything you want, anything. Just don't hurt my baby," I plead.

He chuckles. "Oh, Miss Daniels. If only I had known how agreeable you would be once you got knocked up. I would have taken other measures the first time you were here with me."

He grabs a syringe from his tray and holds it in the air, flicking it until the air bubbles rise to the top. He looks over at Skinny Joe. "Jefferson, I want you to record everything. This is extremely important. Do not miss anything."

Skinny Joe, or Jefferson, I guess, nods emphatically, holding a clipboard and a pen and staring eagerly at the monitors.

"No! No! Don't do this," I am thrashing against my bindings, trying to free myself but it is no use. I am stuck, I have no choice but to lay here and let him do what he wants.

Anderson sticks the needle into the port of my catheter. He injects a small amount as I hold my breath, waiting for the pain, but nothing happens. The room is silent, aside from the two separate sets of beeping coming from the monitors. I look back and forth between Jefferson and Anderson, waiting for someone to say something.

"Second dose," Anderson says, injecting another small amount of liquid.

Still nothing. Minutes pass and nothing happens.

"What's happening?" I ask, hoping against all hope that he gives me something.

"I thought I had it, I really did," he says, but I think he is talking to himself.

"Had what?" I push for an answer.

"Shut up, girl," he snaps, yanking the syringe out of my catheter.

He storms over to the tray and grabs another syringe. "Let's try something more basic," he says, sticking it in my arm. He pushes the plunger just a bit and there is immediate pain. Not the burning fire like before. No, this is like someone is pulling my arms and legs in different directions. Like I am being torn in half because the pain is coming from my midsection. I try to pull my arms and legs back, but they don't move.

I can see Jefferson out of the corner of my eye writing frantically on his clipboard. Both monitors are making so much noise as the lines on the screens bounce erratically. Whatever he gave me is affecting the baby, too.

"Stop!" I plead. "Just stop, please," I cry.

Anderson pulls the needle out and replaces it with another one. After another small injection, the pain stops. "Why are you doing this?" I ask, panting. I am out of breath from screaming and writhing in pain. I honestly don't know how much more of this I can take, and I know he is just starting.

"It's simple, my dear," Anderson starts. He is jotting some notes down in a notebook that he brought in with him. "I am trying to replicate whatever it was that killed all of the women."

That, I was not expecting.

"I don't understand," I say, absolutely confused as to why he would want to do that, why anyone would want to do that.

"Miss Daniels. Use that brain of yours for something other than being a smartass. I work for some very powerful people. And they will pay me big money to be able to recreate the events that happened," he says, but I am still confused.

"Why would someone want to recreate what happened?" I ask, trying to get as much information as I can.

"We all have enemies, my dear. And if someone were to have such a weapon in their arsenal, well... let's just say they would be pretty damn close to invincible," he says simply.

Oh my God. He is trying to weaponize whatever it was that killed everyone.

"The President wants to be able to kill people?" I ask.

"Who said anything about the President?"

"Then who?" I push.

"I think that is enough information for now," he says. "Jefferson, why don't you go and grab our friends? It's time."

Jefferson nods and goes over to the door. He opens it slightly and whispers something to whoever is on the other side. A few seconds later, a large man, one of the goons, comes in. He cracks his knuckles and shakes his hands out.

"What's going on?" I ask, looking at Anderson.

"You see, Miss Daniels. You got me in a lot of trouble when you took off the last time. We found out some interesting facts about you from your blood samples and my employer was very interested in testing my creations on you. You, my dear, have some very unique markers in your blood that make it impossible for diseases to attack your system. I wanted to explore this with you, but you left before I could, and that made me look very bad. So, I feel that we need to... punish you for leaving. Tank, here, is going to help with that punishment. I can't have you leaving this time. I have so much more that I want to do to you as far as testing goes, but first, we are going to have a little fun. Well, Tank is going to have some fun." Anderson is almost giggling with glee. He is so excited about whatever is about to happen.

I look at this big beefcake of a man. He is huge, that's for sure, but there is something dark about him. Something that makes him look evil.

Anderson gathers up his supplies and heads towards the door. Just before he is about to leave, he turns back. "Tank. You are free to do as you wish. Make her hurt, but do not kill her. And nothing in the midsection. I need the fetus to live, at least for now."

Tank just nods. He steps closer to me and runs his fingers down my arm. It causes goosebumps to break out on my skin. I don't know what this man is going to do to me, but I do know that it is not going to be pleasant. His fingers stop at my hand, and he grabs my little finger. Before I can process what is happening, he snaps it to the side, breaking my finger.

I scream, the pain hitting me instantly. I have made it this far in life without breaking a single bone and five seconds alone with this big bastard and that's out the window. But he doesn't stop there, unfortunately. He breaks all the fingers on my right hand with the exception of my thumb. I am screaming in agony, crying, begging him to stop. He doesn't say a word. Doesn't even acknowledge that he heard me.

He leans under the table and turns a knob which makes the table tilt. I am now almost standing, while strapped to the table. He comes to stand in front of me and smirks. He strikes, again, without warning. He backhands me across the face, back and forth, so fast that my head whips back and forth quickly.

I can feel my cheek split open, then my lip. And then, there is nothing.

Chapter 11
The Next Phase
Cassidy

I must have blacked out from the pain because the next thing I know I am being shaken awake.

"No," I say weakly. My voice is cracking, my throat is dry from screaming. "Please, no more," I beg. My hand is throbbing, my face, too. Everything feels swollen. I can barely open my eyes my cheeks are so puffy.

"Cass," someone says. "Cass, honey. Look at me," Jax says, I now recognize his voice.

"Jax?" I ask, not sure I am not hallucinating.

"Yeah, honey. It's me. Damn it! Coop is going to kill me," he says, wiping a damp cloth across my forehead. "I can't clean you up too much or they'll know that I was here. Talk to me, Cass. What's been going on?"

I feel like I am going to throw up. I am lying flat on the table again. Someone must have repositioned me after Tank finished beating me.

"Well, let's see," I start, but have a hard time enunciating because of how swollen my face is. "I had an amazing reunion with Anderson and his wonderful concoction of torture liquids. Then, this behemoth named Tank came in and beat the hell out of me after he broke all the fingers on my right hand. Oh wait, no. He missed my thumb," I say with as much venom as I can muster right now.

"I'm so sorry, Cass. I wish I could get you out of here," he says, sounding really upset. I just sigh, knowing full well that I can't leave. Not when Anderson has started giving me some information.

"It's ok, Jax. It's not your fault," I tell him because it's not. "Listen. I know we don't have much time," I start, stopping because I have to gag.

All I can taste in my mouth is blood. I lean as much to the side, away from Jax, and empty my stomach. I must have swallowed a lot of blood while I was out. Thank goodness I didn't drown in my own blood.

Jax wipes my mouth when I'm done. "Thanks. Sorry," I say, trying not to throw up again.

"It's ok, Cass. Really, it's ok," he says, wiping my forehead again.

"Anyway, you have to tell the General that Anderson is trying to recreate whatever it was that wiped everyone out. He is trying to weaponize it. I don't know who he is working for. The only thing he said is that they are very powerful people but it's not the President," I explain in a rush. I'm starting to feel like I am going to black out again and there is more I have to tell him.

"But what is his obsession with you?" Jax asks.

"He said he found something in my blood that makes it hard for disease to affect me. He needs me to test his creations. I guess if it affects me... it is good," I say, now knowing that I am truly going to die.

He looks up at the monitors and then back down at me, frowning. "I heard," he says. "I'm so sorry, Cass. I'm sorry that you had to find out here. I was hoping that it was just a rumor, but..." he trails off.

I choke back the sob that is threatening its way out. "I wish things were different," I whisper, knowing that he will understand. He was with Cooper and me back in the beginning. He is a part of our story.

"Cooper is going to rescue you, Cass. I know it. Especially once he finds out you are pregnant," Jax tells me, trying to reassure me. Little does he know, all that does is fire me up even more.

"Jax. No matter what happens, you can't let Cooper know that I am pregnant. That I died with his child in me. He will never recover from that," I beg, tears running down my face now.

"Oh, honey," he says sadly. "God, Cass. If there was any way for me to change this, to make it so that this never happened, I would. I would take your place if I could," he says, wiping my tears. He looks at me and wipes away a few of my tears. "You are going to make the most amazing mother."

God, how I wish that were true. I wish that this was another one of my bad dreams. I wish that any second now, I would wake up safe, in Cooper's arms. But that is not going to happen.

"There's just one thing I don't understand. Why does he hate you so much?" Jax asks.

I choke down the rest of my tears and take a deep breath. "Apparently, I got him in a lot of trouble when I escaped. His employer was not happy with him. So, Tank was my punishment."

Jax grazes my broken hand lightly and I wince. I need to lighten the mood. "But seriously though, tell me. How do I look?" I joke.

"Don't joke about that, Cass. It's bad enough when I tell Cooper what they did to you."

"You can't tell him, Jax! You can't tell him what they are doing to me. He'll get himself killed trying to get me out," I almost shout, but quickly remember where I am and that I can't get Jax in trouble.

He sighs and looks at me for a long time. "Ok, Cass. I won't. But this has to end soon, or he will kill you."

They are going to kill me anyway, but I don't say that.

"Just tell them I am ok. That's all they need to know," I say.

The door slams open and Jax quickly recovers by grabbing one of the ties holding my hands to the table and making it look like he was tightening it.

"What are you doing in here?" Anderson asks him sharply. "You're supposed to be guarding the door."

"I heard her thrashing around and I came to check her ties," he says quickly.

Anderson seems to buy this and tells Jax to go. Jax nods and leaves, again without a second glance at me.

"I have a couple more serums to try with you, Miss Daniels. I'm glad that you're awake," Anderson tells me, dragging his tray of syringes over to my side.

"What, your little assistant is too busy to help this time?"

"Oh, I have Jefferson busy in the lab. I can do this test myself," he says, giving me his best evil-scientist smile.

He picks up the first syringe and sticks it into the port in my arm. Everything is already throbbing and I can't imagine how much more pain I could feel right now.

I was wrong. He injects the liquid, the entire contents of the syringe this time, and I immediately feel a stabbing pain behind my eyes. My vision cuts out like someone flipped a switch. I try to scream, I really do, but I can't even move the pain is so severe. I squeeze my eyes closed and groan. It's all I can get out. The beeping on the monitors goes crazy.

"Good, good. We are getting closer," he mumbles to himself, writing in his notebook.

"I can't see, you asshole! What did you give me?" I ask, breathing heavily. I blink my eyes rapidly, as if that will clear my vision, but all I see is black. I know my eyes are open, I can feel it, but he just made me blind.

"Just another test, Miss Daniels. I'm just glad to see that you aren't immune to everything," he says, and I can tell he is smiling even though I can't see it.

I can hear him scribbling in his notebook.

"One more. She can handle one more," he whispers as if he is talking to himself. "But which one? I can't kill her, at least not yet. I'll try serum four fifty-three next. Shouldn't be too bad."

He pulls on my hand to straighten my arm and I scream. He grabbed my broken fingers. He doesn't seem to care because he doesn't let go. I can feel my bones moving, and I'm pretty sure that's not supposed to happen.

"Now, Miss Daniels, you have to tell me what you feel with this one," he says.

I know exactly when he injects the liquid because I get an ice-cold feeling that starts at the catheter and slowly makes its way up my arm. It spreads throughout my entire body, making me feel like someone just dipped my body into a frozen river. I don't know if you know just how badly this type of coldness hurts, but it is beyond what I can describe.

I manage to scream and beg him to stop. This is becoming a pattern. I hear him laughing, apparently pleased with himself.

"Very nice. This is perfect!"

The last thing I remember is the door slamming, and I am out again.

Chapter 12

Bad News

Cooper

It's been thirty-six hours since she was taken. A day and a half since I heard her voice, or felt her kiss. And almost two days, that she has been in his possession. It hurts to even imagine what she is going through, how much pain she is in. What's worse, is the fact that I am just sitting here with my thumb up my ass, not doing a damn thing. I'm not allowed to, because the General ordered me to do nothing.

We haven't had an update from Jax since she first got there. I know that Jax will get word to us when he can, but it kills me to just sit idly by and wait. I was not built for this. I was built for action, especially when it comes to defending the woman I love.

Austin and I are sitting with the General, going over the plans for the facility, for the hundredth time. We have determined the best points of entry, the guard rotation, and pretty much everything else that would give us the best opportunity to take it down. We are just waiting for word from Jax that we are a go.

A knock at the door stops the General mid-sentence. "Come in," he says loudly.

A young man enters carrying a piece of paper, hands it to the General, and then quickly leaves.

"It's an update from Jax," he says, which causes me to jump out of my chair.

"What does it say?" I all but shout at him.

He doesn't answer right away. Just as I am about to jump over his desk and rip the paper out of his hands, he looks up.

"I can't believe it. She did it. She got what we needed, well, almost what we need," he says, with no further explanation.

I look at him. "General, please," I beg.

"Oh, sorry. She is ok. Still alive. There is no information about what they are doing to her, but she found out that Anderson is trying to recreate whatever it was that started all of this. He is working for some people, not the President, to weaponize it," he explains.

"That's all well and good, sir, but what exactly does it say about Cassidy," I yell, frustrated that I have to drag it out of him.

He hands me the note to read for myself.

Cassidy is ok. She said to tell Cooper and Austin that she is fine. Anderson

intends to recreate the origin. He has been hired by some powerful people

to weaponize it – he is not working for the President. He is testing on Cassidy,

but so far, she is still alive. He told Cassidy she is somehow immune to

this thing. She wants Cooper and Austin to hold tight. She thinks she can

get more from Anderson. Will send more info soon.

That's it? That's all he can tell us about how Cassidy is doing? "Sir, if he is testing on her, it is only a matter of time before whatever he is giving her kills her. We have to move now. This is more than enough to go on!"

"Soldier, I suggest you watch your tone with me. I have been more than forgiving of your insubordination because of the situation. But don't expect my tolerance to continue much longer," he warns me. "We have to find out who he is working for. That is the most important thing. If we don't, and we take Anderson, they will just find someone else to do their bidding."

I just nod, not capable of saying anything right now or I will go and get myself in trouble. How can he just ignore the fact that Cassidy is being used as a lab rat? I look at Austin and nod toward the door.

"Sir? I think I am going to take Cooper outside to get some air. Can we check in with you later?" Austin asks him.

He is so lost in reading and re-reading the note that he just nods at him without looking up. Austin and I make our way out of the room. I am beyond livid right now, so I don't dare speak until we are outside and completely clear of the building. Austin leads me over to the edge of the woods.

"What the fuck is wrong with him!" I shout.

"Cooper, you have to keep it together, man. I am worried about her, too," he starts, but I cut him off.

"Are you! Are you really, Aus? Because you sure as hell aren't acting like it," I spit at him.

I don't see the punch coming because I am too busy pacing back and forth, but he hits me square in the jaw, and it hurts like hell.

"Don't you dare!" he growls at me. "That is my sister! I am pissed beyond belief that we didn't storm that place right away. I am just using my head, unlike you. You keep going around screaming and throwing little temper tantrums to the General and you are going to get yourself kicked off the base, or worse. I am worried, Cooper. I am so worried that I haven't slept more than a couple of hours since we've been back. Fuck! He is experimenting on my baby sister and there is nothing I can do about it."

It isn't until he finishes that I finally stop and take my head out of my ass and really look at him. Austin has black circles under his eyes, his hair is a mess, and he looks bad. I have been so caught up in my own head that I haven't stopped to consider how he is dealing with all of this.

"I'm sorry, Aus. I... I just can't... what if something happens to her?" I all but choke out, fighting back the sob that is threatening its way up my throat. "I can't lose her."

"I can't either. And that is exactly why we are going to bust our asses doing everything we can to make this mission a success. I am not coming back without Cassidy. Let me rephrase that, I am not coming back without my sister alive."

I nod in complete agreement. Now, we just have to figure out how we are going to do just that.

Chapter 13
Death Warmed Over

Cassidy

I'm sure you've heard the saying before, but I feel like death warmed over. I woke up a few minutes ago because my head was pounding. My hand feels so swollen it could pass for a boxing glove, not to mention I can't move it at all. I'm afraid to open my eyes. I don't want to know if I am still blind. Everything on my body hurts. I don't feel the freezing cold anymore, just blinding pain. I decide to get it over with and open my eyes. Pitch black, I still can't see. I can only hope that it isn't permanent. Stupid. Of course, I guess it doesn't really matter, does it? He's going to kill me soon. It's only a matter of time.

The only thing that brings me solace right now is the rapid little beating of my baby's heart. I have no idea what all of this is doing to my poor little bean. I'm sure it can't be good. I feel a tear run down my cheek. Well, I guess the tear ducts are still working. Somehow, that doesn't bring me much relief. I have no idea how long I have been here or what day it is. It feels like a lifetime. What I wouldn't give to feel Cooper's arms wrapped around me right now. I just hope that Jax was able to pass the information along. And I sure as hell hope it helps in the cause.

After a little bit, I hear the door open. I wait, holding my breath, for someone to say something but it is silent. Maybe this is another one of Anderson's tactics, messing with my head. I certainly wouldn't put it past him.

After a few minutes, I hear what sounds like sniffling.

"Who's there?" I croak out, my throat still scratchy from screaming.

I feel a gentle touch on my arm. "It's me, Cassidy," Shelby says quietly.

"Shelby?" I ask.

"Yeah. I'm right here," she says, turning my head gently so I am looking in her direction. "Oh, God, Cassidy. I'm so sorry," she sobs.

I blink rapidly, trying like hell to get my vision to work, but it isn't happening. "What are you sorry for, Shelby? None of this is your fault," I say, trying to soothe her with my words since I can't touch her.

"If only you could see what you look like right now," she says.

I feel a cool, wet cloth gently on my face. "What are you doing? You're going to get in trouble. Get out of here," I say in a rush, not wanting any of this to happen to her.

"It's ok. They sent me in here to clean you up and feed you. He said he wants you to keep your strength up," she explains, continuing to clean me.

She is silent for a while, I'm sure she's focusing on her task. I can't even imagine what I look like.

"Shelby?"

"What is it, Cassidy?"

"What do I look like right now?"

She sniffles and I feel a tear drop hit my arm. "You don't want to know," she says, going back to cleaning.

"I do, though. I really do. I think I need to know. I need something to fuel my hatred for him. It will keep me fighting."

I thought I was prepared to know, but I was wrong.

"Both of your eyes are swollen, and black and blue. Your lip is split in several places. You have blood coming from your mouth. You must have some cuts on your head because there is blood matted in your hair. And your right hand and arm are swollen. Your fingers," she trails off.

"My fingers, what, Shelby?"

She clears her throat. "Your fingers are bent in the wrong direction."

She goes back to cleaning me but continues to cry. I know she is crying because I occasionally feel a tear hit my arms and she sniffles every few seconds.

I have more to ask her, but I am scared.

"Shelby. Please tell me my baby is ok." I know the monitor is still beeping, but that is the extent of my knowledge.

"The heart rate is steady, but that's all I know. I wish I could tell you more."

She finishes her little sponge bath. Next, she brings me some water. It hurts to drink but also feels good. My throat is so scratchy and dry.

"Is it true you can't see?" she asks me after a few minutes.

"Yeah. But don't you worry about me. I can take whatever he throws at me," I say, trying to sound strong. The last thing I want is her worrying about me. I'm doing enough of that for both of us.

She tries to get me to eat, but it hurts too much to chew right now. She promises to bring me soup the next time she comes. If there is a next time.

We don't get much time together before I hear the door open again. "That's enough, girl. Get out," I hear one of the goons say. "This isn't the Four Seasons. The doc said to clean her up and get her to eat a little. That's it."

Shelby apologizes quietly to me and promises to come back soon.

"Watch how you talk to her," I say to the goon. He has no right to talk to her like that.

"It's ok, Cassidy. Really," Shelby says quietly as she rushes from the room.

I hear what sounds like stomping and the next thing I know my hand is being squeezed. I scream, able to produce quite a bit of sound now that I had something to drink.

"Enough," Anderson says sharply. "I need her alert. You'll make her pass out again."

I stop screaming when he lets go of my hand. There is so much pain, that I can almost feel the broken bones. I wish I could see him right now. I wish I could make him hurt. The only good thing about this is that I know exactly how to get under his skin. "Awe," I manage to say. "Are you worried about me? How sweet," I say to Anderson.

"Watch it, Miss Daniels."

The door closes loudly which I'm assuming is because the goon slammed it in anger. Well, at least I can still get under someone's skin.

"So, what's next?" I ask Anderson, my voice is raw, scratchy. I know he is still in the room because I can smell him. I never really noticed before, probably because I was so focused on how he looked like a doozer from Fraggle Rock, but he has a distinct odor to him. Kind of like Lysol mixed with a big turd.

"Oh, we have some more testing to do," he says from right next to me.

"Oh goody."

He grabs a fist full of my hair and yanks hard. "Don't test me, Miss Daniels. I am almost finished with my testing. You don't want to know what I plan next."

He releases my hair just as quickly as he grabbed it. It feels like he ripped a bunch of my hair out. I feel him tap my arm. I can tell when he sticks the needle in because my catheter moves just a bit. "Let me know what you think of this one," he says, and I can tell he is smiling by the sound of his voice. It really is amazing how heightened your other senses become when you lose one of them.

I don't feel anything right away and I wonder if he hasn't injected it yet. Then, all of a sudden, it feels like my skin is melting, right where the catheter is located. I cry out and scramble, trying to free my arm. I hear Anderson cursing and calling for help, and then the door slams open. I think a few more people have entered the room because there is a lot of rustling around me. There is a lot of shouting, and I can feel several people touching me. There are people holding me down while someone yanks the catheter out of my arm. It feels like they are pouring some kind of thick gel all over my arm. It soothes the pain a little, but I am still screaming. I don't know what he just injected, but I do know that it did not have the intended effect.

I feel someone yanking on my other arm. They put in yet another catheter. I feel injection after injection in that catheter and in the muscles in my arms and legs. I'm guessing they are trying to counteract whatever it was that he gave me.

I hear Anderson barking orders, I hear Jefferson's voice as well, mixed in with the shouting. They are frantic. I try to listen for the beating of my baby's heart, just to focus on something, but there is so much commotion that I can't pick it out. If that small injection was able to melt my skin and cause this much trouble, I'm sure it wasn't good for the baby.

After what feels like forever, things start to calm down. The pain has dulled, but it is still there.

"What... what did you do to me?" I ask no one in particular.

Of course, no one answers me. Why would they? I mean, they only just about melted my arm off. Why would I need to know what is going on? Assholes.

After a while, I can tell that everyone left the room. I hear a slow drip. I think they hooked me up to some kind of fluids. I try to move my arm, but that only causes me more pain, so I just lay still. I think they covered my new wound in a bandage. My arm feels weird, not right. I have no idea what just happened other than it wasn't planned. I have no idea what my arm looks like right now, but if it looks even half as bad as it feels, I'm in trouble.

I decide that now is as good a time as any to try to rest. Whatever just happened shook them up, that much is for sure. I should take advantage of the time alone. I take some deep breaths. I try to focus on the beeping of the monitors. Mine is a steady loud beep.

I focus on the other beeping, the quicker one. Only now, it doesn't sound quite as fast as it was before, and that scares the ever-living hell out of me.

Chapter 14
Nightmares Come to Life
Cassidy

The days are blending together now. Time no longer exists. It's just one big blur of pain. I can't even tell you how many different serums Anderson has tried on me. The only thing I can tell you is that I think I am becoming immune to the pain. I don't feel anything anymore. The highlight of my day is when they let Shelby come in to clean me up and feed me. I have been able to eat small amounts of soup each time. If I eat too much, I get sick. I wish I could say it is from morning sickness, but I think it is really the serums that are getting to me.

The only thing I am concerned about at this point is the baby. As long as I can hear that beeping, I know my little bean is still with me. My vision has started to return a little bit. I can see a little bit of light and shapes, but that's about it.

I hear the door open and look over to see a small shape enter the room. Shelby.

"Hey, Shelby."

"Hey, Cassidy. How are you feeling today?"

"I'm ok. I can see a little bit more each day, so I've got that going for me," I joke.

She starts to untie my arms and legs. "What are you doing?" I whisper loudly.

"It's ok, Cassidy. They are letting me take you to the shower today."

I haven't been on my feet for more than the few minutes that it has taken me to pee in the last few days. And as much as it embarrasses me to say, I didn't have to get up to do that much because most of the time, I wet myself during the testing. They have taken so much of my blood in the last few days. Each time they tried a new serum, they took blood. They have also been taking samples of my amniotic fluid to test how the serums are affecting the baby. I keep having nightmares that when I have the baby, it is born with extra limbs, or completely deformed. It scares me.

Shelby unties me and helps me sit up. I have to sit there for a few minutes, waiting for the nausea and dizziness to pass. When I finally get up, my legs are weak, and unstable. It takes us a long time to make it to the shower room. No one helps us, of course, not that I would expect any of these savages to lend a hand. I have to stop several times because of shooting pain in my arm, my head, and my abdomen. I am really concerned about that last one, but who can I tell at this point? No one will care.

When she finally gets me to the shower, she has to help me strip down. I am only wearing a hospital gown at this point. They had to change me too many times after I had accidents that they gave up on clothes and put me in gowns. I have no modesty anymore. So many of the doctors and scientists have had their hands in my junk that I just don't care. She gets me situated in the shower with a stool to sit on and then leaves me alone. The hot water feels amazing. I feel a stinging sensation in my right arm and look down at it. I still can't see very well, but I can see enough to know that my arm is not supposed to look the way that it does right now. My flesh is torn to shreds and it looks like a went a few rounds with a wolverine. That must be from the one serum that had Anderson so upset. My hand is completely disfigured, my fingers crooked and swollen like Vienna sausages.

I take my time, not so much cleaning myself as just standing under the water. I didn't think I would get to feel this again after the last time. I was sure this would be a privilege I wouldn't get. But I guess even the worst people have a slightly decent side.

When I finally turn the water off, Shelby is right there with a towel to dry me off. We are just about to put a fresh hospital gown on when I feel wet between my legs.

"Shelby. Didn't we dry my legs?" I ask, unsure now if we did or not.

"We did. It's... oh my God, Cassidy. You're bleeding," she cries loudly. "Stay here. I'll go get help!"

She runs from the room, screaming for help over and over again. All I can do is stand there, bleeding. I feel a big gush and look down to see a large pool of blood between my feet on the floor. It is running down my legs. Within a few seconds, Shelby is back with Anderson and a few of the goons.

"Grab her! Get her to the study room, now!" Anderson barks.

One of the goons scoops me into his arms. It feels like I am being held by a brick wall this man is so hard. It is a bumpy ride as he runs down the hall with me. When we make it to the room, I am immediately placed on the table as people rush around me, hooking me back up to the machines and fluids. I look around, trying desperately to see faces so I can try and read the situation. I may not know a lot about being pregnant, but I know enough that bleeding isn't good.

I hear the first monitor jump to life. It is fast but steady. My heartbeat. I wait, anxiously, for the second monitor, for the sound of life from inside me. Seconds go by. Then minutes. But nothing.

"Try a different position," Anderson says, and the probes are repositioned.

Still nothing.

"Get me the ultrasound, now!"

More rushing about, the door opening and closing, people shouting out in the hallway.

"What's going on, Anderson? Is my baby ok?" I beg, not really sure I want to know the answer.

"Shut up, girl," he snaps.

I hear a machine being wheeled in, the ultrasound. Warm goop is dumped onto my belly and then the probe is there.

Still nothing.

Silence.

Maddening silence.

"Someone tell me what the fuck is going on!" I shout to no one in particular.

A chuckle, from Anderson, I'm sure. "I apologize, Miss Daniels. It seems that I have killed your baby."

A deafening scream is heard. I realize it's me. I jump up from the table because they never tied me back down. I dive at Anderson, wanting to kill him, but I don't get far. I am grabbed by a pair of meaty hands and slammed into the wall. I hear the crunch of my nose breaking and feel my hand crunching as he has it pinned behind my back. I am still screaming, wailing. The sobs that are coming from me are loud, and messy. The sounds coming out of me right now are out of pain, but it's not physical. It is the emotional pain that a mother feels when they lose their child. It is a pain worse than anything Anderson has done to me.

My baby is gone. I lost it. No, it was taken from me. He knew damned well what he was doing.

"You knew, you bastard! You knew what you were giving me would kill him," I scream at the top of my lungs. If I can't physically hurt him, maybe my words can do some damage. "You lost your daughter! You know what it is like to lose a child and yet you still did this to me! You evil bastard!" I sob uncontrollably. My little bean. My last piece of Cooper is gone.

My head is slammed against the wall. "I warned you, Miss Daniels. I told you what would happen if you brought my daughter up again."

I barely hear him because of the ringing in my ears. He slammed my head hard and my head is buzzing.

"Tie her down. And make sure she can't move at all," he tells the goon holding me.

I am roughly moved back over to the table. I don't fight this time. My fight is gone. Just like my baby.

Once I'm tied down, I just lay there crying.

"Shut up, Miss Daniels. You are making a scene," Anderson tells me.

"Why don't you just kill me? Why keep dragging it out? You know you are going to eventually. Just put me out of my misery," I spit at him.

"Oh, now Miss Daniels. I can't do that. My boss would be extremely disappointed in me if I killed you now. We are so close to recreating it. So very close."

"What? Does your terrorist boss care about one female? I find that hard to believe. I find it extremely hard to believe that some foreign terrorist cares about me at all," I taunt him. I know I should just keep my mouth shut but I just don't care anymore. I'm as good as dead. I know that now more than ever.

I must have pushed a button because he slams his hands down on the table, on either side of my head.

"How dare you call our Vice President a terrorist! What he is doing is securing our nation's future. Do you realize that the United States would be invincible if the rest of the world knew that we could recreate the event? No one would dare touch us, or come near us out of fear of losing their people. Nuclear weapons are officially a thing of the past. This... what I am doing is making the United States the most powerful nation in the world," he rants.

I don't think he realizes that he just gave me the last piece of information that we need. He is working for the Vice President. Our Vice President. That explains why the facilities have been able to function. They are operating under the orders of the government, just not the President.

I don't dare say anything else, because I have to live long enough to get this information to Jax so that he can pass it on to the General.

Anderson turns to look at me. "What's the matter, Miss Daniels? Did I finally shock you? Not what you were expecting?"

I shake my head slightly and close my eyes, willing him to just leave me alone. Usually, Jax comes to see me after Anderson is done with me for the day.

"Well, in light of our most recent events, I am feeling generous. I have some more work to do in the lab and I need you to heal up a bit before our next round of testing, so we are going to call it a day," he sing-songs like he is doing me a favor.

"What? So soon?" I deadpan, internally hitting myself for not keeping my mouth shut like I just said I was going to. I just can't help it sometimes.

He just glares at me, and I glare back. He gives first and turns to leave. "Do try and heal fast, Miss Daniels. I have big plans for you tomorrow."

Finally, he is gone, and I can mourn the loss of my baby in peace. I cry for a long time. At least now, Cooper will never have to know. I made Jax promise not to tell him, and I know Shelby will keep quiet as well. She and I talked about it at length one day. I told her that I knew I was going to die. Cooper was going to have a hard enough time with that, I don't want to add to that by telling him that he also lost our son.

I don't know why I keep saying he and calling it a boy. Some part of me just knows.

I must have dozed off at some point because the next thing I know I am being shaken awake by Jax.

"Cassidy, honey. Wake up," he says quietly.

I blink my eyes rapidly, trying to clear my vision, but it is still messed up. I can make out the outline of his face, but no details.

"Jax. Thank God you're here," I say. "I have more information for the General."

"Hold on, Cass. Are you ok? I heard about the baby, honey. I'm so sorry," he says, touching my arm gently.

I fight back the sob. I don't have time to break down right now. I promise myself a good cry once he leaves, but for now, I have to tell him what I know.

"I'm... ok, Jax. But listen. I found out who he is working for, I found out who his boss is. He is working directly for the Vice President. He thinks by weaponizing this thing, that he can make the U.S. the most powerful nation in the world. He thinks other nations will cower to us knowing that we can recreate everything. You have to tell the General. You have to get that news out now," I say as fast as I can.

"Ok, honey. I'll tell them. Calm down," he tries to soothe me.

"No, Jax. I can't. That's the last piece. I know that is the last thing the General needs to know to take this place down."

"I know, Cass. I can't do anything until tomorrow morning. I am on guard duty all night. Once I am off, I will send word. I promise," he vows.

That isn't exactly what I want to hear, that he has to wait all night, but it's something.

"Cass. How are you, really?"

I feel the tears before I realize I am crying. "I lost him, Jax," I sob. "Anderson killed him. My little bean is gone and it's all his fault. He was a little piece of Cooper. A piece of me. And now he is nothing. It's like I never really had him."

"Awe, Cass. He was real, and he was both you and Cooper. No one can take that away from you. He will always be a part of you, he will just be in your heart now. And Cooper's," Jax says.

"No, Jax. You can't ever tell Cooper. It will kill him!"

"Cassidy, you can't keep this alone. It will kill you to hold this secret," he tries to convince me.

"But that's just it, Jax. I am dead either way. At least as far as Cooper is concerned, he is only losing me. And that's more than enough."

Jax starts to tell me I'm wrong, but I cut him off. "I'm really sorry, Jax. But I think I just need to be alone right now. Please just go," I cry.

He starts to say something but stops. "Ok, Cass. But I'll be right outside if you need me."

He closes the door quietly behind him, and I am left alone to mourn the loss of my baby and my future.

Chapter 15
The Final Piece of the Puzzle
Cooper

She did it. She figured out who Anderson is working for, and we are nothing short of shocked. Now, my only focus is getting her out of there. Austin and I are on our way to the General's office to finalize our plans for the takedown. I am almost running to get there because the sooner we get this planned, the sooner we can be on our way.

We pass a bunch of people in the hallways who stop to salute us. We get to his office and find the rest of our team already there. It is the same group we always go with. I know it's rude, but I bypass everyone and head straight for the General.

"Sir," I say while saluting him.

"Have a seat Staff Sergeant. We are ready to get started," he says.

We all take our seats and stare at the General.

"I know some of you know this, but we got the final piece of information from Jax this morning. We are ready to start our mission. I need everyone on point for this one, not that you haven't been up to this point. This is the big one, the one we've been waiting for since this started. If we can do this, if we can capture Anderson, the rest of the facilities will be on their own and weaker, easier to take down."

Everyone nods in agreement. The General looks at me next. "Cooper... I think you should sit this one out," he starts, as I jump up from my seat to argue. "Hear me out, soldier. You are too close to this you will be compromised in your decision-making."

"No offense, sir, but over my dead body will I stay behind. Court martial me or do whatever you need to, but I *am* going!" I say emphatically.

"Cooper," Austin starts but I shoot him a look that says it all.

There is nothing on heaven or earth that could stop me. I am going to get my woman. The General just nods, accepting that he is not going to win this one. I don't care what they do to me, I really don't. I would give up my entire military career, hell, my life for Cassidy.

The meeting continues as we go over the plan. Wheels up tomorrow morning. Twelve more hours until I can finally be in action. I've had enough of this sitting around and waiting bull shit. I am not built for waiting. Never was.

When we are finally dismissed, I storm out of the room. I am on a mission. I want to get my gear ready. I am walking quickly down the hall when I hear Austin shouting my name.

"Coop, wait up!"

I slow just slightly so that he can catch up to me. He walks silently next to me until we are out of the building. Once we are outside, he steers me over toward the woods again.

"What's up, man? I want to go get my gear ready," I say impatiently, pacing back and forth.

He sighs. "Coop, maybe you should consider what the General said."

My eyes dart up to his and I immediately stop.

"I know you did not just say that," I growl.

"Listen, Coop. You aren't in the right mind to do this. We need to focus on the mission as well as saving Cass. I know you, and I know that when we get there you will have one purpose, and one purpose only, and that's getting to Cassidy. These men, our brothers that are going with us need to be able to depend on you to have their backs and if you are only there for Cassidy... well, that's just not fair to them."

I consider what he is saying for about half a second. "You're wrong, Austin, and quite frankly, it pisses me off that you would even think that. I am a Marine. I would never leave any of my brothers hanging like that. Yes, my main priority is getting to Cassidy, but I also understand what this mission is all about. This is what we have been working for.

This is for the big picture. Anderson must be stopped. And I will be the one to put the bullet between his eyes."

"See, that's exactly what I am saying. We have to take Anderson alive. We can't go in there and kill him or that defeats the purpose of the whole thing. He needs to be interrogated for more information. Cassidy has done her job in getting us the basics, but we need more in order to stop this whole thing. You think that Vice President Thompson is the only one in on this? I can guarantee you he isn't. There are probably a bunch of governmental officials in on this plot. And we need to know how far this goes."

He stops to let this sink in before he continues. "Coop, I want to save Cassidy, too. No, I need to. But unfortunately, she is not the priority. She has to be the secondary." A tear runs down his cheek. "Coop, if something happens to her, I will never forgive myself. Never. But because of everything, because of what everyone is going through right now, we owe it to them to do the right thing."

I look at him, slightly shocked at what he is saying. He is saying that our mission is more important than his sister. And I know he thinks that's the way it has to be. I know that he doesn't want to lose Cass either. But I am not going to sit here and agree with him.

"I know you mean well, Aus. I really do. But I can't agree with you on this one."

"Cooper, we don't have a choice," he says.

"You may not have a choice, Austin. But I do. If we can't save her, if we don't make her our priority over everything else, then what the hell are we fighting for in the first place? She is not only your sister, and the love of my life, but she is a viable female. And they have been our priority since day one. Open your eyes, man. This has gone so far beyond just being a Marine at this point. We are human beings, fighting for our survival. And she is the key to that."

I walk away because I just can't talk to him right now. Not when he is going to try and stop me from going. I will admit that I will try my hardest to get to Cassidy once we get there. But for him to suggest that I will ignore my duties is insulting. I always keep my head. I am going to save her, because honestly, I don't know what I will do if I can't.

Chapter 16
The Beginning of the End
Cassidy

Anderson is cleaning up his supplies having just finished with his testing for the day. Shelby told me earlier that I have been here for ten days. Ten days he has been using me as his personal guinea pig. I hate to admit it, but I have been praying that one of the serums would kill me. I knew he would torture me if I came back, I just never thought it would be this bad. My insides feel like someone took a blender and mixed them all up. I have lost weight, a lot of weight. My ribs are sticking out, and my hip bones are visible. I haven't been able to eat much of anything, just some liquids here and there. They have been pumping fluids into me, trying to keep me alive for as long as possible. Anderson is close in his research. Each serum brings me more and more pain and agony. He said that the more pain and anguish he causes me means that he is that much closer to the end. My end, he means. Or maybe not. I can't even think anymore. My head just throbs constantly. My vision was almost back to normal but then I lost it again after one of the serums. He thinks it's because there is inflammation in my brain, pressure on my optic nerve, or something like that. I don't know much about the human anatomy, just the little bit of first aid that Austin taught me. So maybe he's telling the truth. All I know is that some days I can see, and some I can't.

I am in and out most of the time. Not even the pain is enough to wake me up. I am just dying, slowly. I wouldn't wish this on my worst enemy. No, not even Anderson. What he has put me through is more than any one person should ever have to feel. Jax still comes to see me, but I am barely able to open my eyes when he is here. He just talks to me softly and tells me how Cooper is coming for me. I haven't spoken in days having lost the ability a while ago. There is just no fight left in me. I am waiting to die.

The only thing keeping me going is the slight chance that I could see Cooper one last time before I die. Maybe, just maybe, I could survive long enough for him and Austin to come for me. I wouldn't be able to tell them that I love them, but I want that picture in my head when I go. The two people who love me most in the world.

It's about time for Jax to come in, Anderson left a while ago. I lay here waiting for him, but he doesn't show. He hasn't missed a day yet, so I start to worry that something happened to him. I don't have long to worry as I hear a commotion outside the door. I can hear people running down the hall, shouting about men and guns.

Then, an explosion rocks the building. The floor shakes and pieces of ceiling drop around me. I use all my energy to turn my head and look at the door. I don't dare hope that this is our men making their attempt at the facility. I wouldn't want to be let down just in case it isn't. The door to my room slams against the wall and a very dirty Shelby enters. She runs right over to me and covers my body I'm assuming to protect me from the falling debris.

"Cassidy! Cassidy! Look at me!" she begs.

I blink my eyes slowly and try to focus on her face. I can only make out the shape of her, no details. It is dark, or at least my vision is. The lights are flickering, that much I can tell.

The next thing I know, Anderson and a few of his men rush into the room. "Quick! We have to get her out of here. They are coming to take her," he shouts.

The men quickly start untying me, and I am scooped up into hard arms. Shelby tries to fight them. I can hear her screaming and feel her pulling on my good arm. I feel her grip on my arm slip and I am rushed from the room. They are running, fast. I have no idea where they are taking me. I couldn't fight them if I tried. I hear the gunfire and then another explosion, this one closer. We are in a stairwell, but I can't tell if we are going up or down. Doors are slammed, more shouting and some shots are fired behind us. I am having trouble staying awake. I fight the darkness that is trying to consume me. I wish I could make out faces to see if I recognize anyone. I think most of the people that we have passed are those that work here, none of our guys.

They finally settle in a room and close the door. I am unceremoniously tossed in the corner. I fall into a lump on the floor, my arms and legs a tangled mess.

"Guard the door! No one gets in!" Anderson shouts.

The door slams again and I can only assume that the goons are standing guard as he just instructed. I try to open my eyes and focus to try and see who is in the room. The only person I can make out for sure, because of his smell, is Anderson himself.

"I won't let them take you," he snarls. "I'm so close, so close. I have to finish, or they'll kill me." He is talking more to himself, his voice is fading and getting louder, indicating that he is pacing back and forth. I try to move my arms and legs so that I am more comfortable, but it's no use. I'm stuck.

I have no idea how long we are in here. The sound of the fighting has faded. That's it. They aren't coming for me. I won't get to see Cooper or Austin before I die. This is the last thought that I have before it all goes dark.

Chapter 17
Taking It Down

Cooper

I t's finally time. We are at the rendezvous point right outside of the facility in Washington, D.C. We are waiting for the signal from the Chipmunks, as Cassidy would call them. They will signal us to make our move with the first explosion. With all the intel from Jax, we were able to determine that they have amped up their security since they detained Cassidy.

It is dusk, right before the last guard change of the day. Attacking at this point doesn't necessarily give us the advantage, but it should cause some confusion. I am with the Alpha team, with Austin right behind me. I am not the leader of this mission and they deemed me unfit for command because of my connection to Cassidy. Austin is second in command, under Sergeant Major John Kipper, or as we call him, Kip.

They are doing communications checks right now, with Private Trottman. I have been finding it hard to be around him since Cassidy was taken. I don't blame him, per se, but I kind of do. It's childish. I know he did everything he could to protect her. He even got injured in the process.

"Cooper, radio check," Trottman says into my ear.

"Check," I say, not being able to muster anything else up.

Austin shoots me a look, which I ignore.

We wait in silence for the signal. I find my mind wandering, like it always does, to Cassidy. The pain in my chest has been constant since she was taken. She is already part of my soul. I try to focus on the positives, like what we will do once all of this is over. I can picture our wedding day and how beautiful she will look. I can see her smile as she walks down the aisle, right into my arms. Austin will give her away. It won't be a big wedding, just a few of our closest friends. The only family will be Austin.

After the ceremony, we will dance and eat and celebrate with our friends. That night, though, that night is just for the two of us. I will make love to her, hold her in my arms all night. Then, the next day, we will disappear. I don't care where we go, I just want her alone for as long as we can get. Maybe we will go to my cabin, maybe a beach somewhere. As long as it is just us. I picture us making a life at my cabin. Having children. God, I can't wait for her to get pregnant. She will make the most amazing mother. I want to have a bunch of kids, a really big family. I didn't have a family growing us so nothing would bring me more joy than to have a loving family with Cassidy.

Of course, this is all dependent upon us saving her.

An explosion brings me back to reality. I hear Kip shouting go into the radio, so I jump to my feet and take off. We are entering the prison through the south side. The first explosion took place on the opposite side, so as not to cause damage where we are entering. Another team is taking the front entrance, and the final team is on the west entrance. We drop smoke as soon as we are inside to hide our advance. We immediately encounter a small group of guards. They shoot first and we counter with our own shots. It lasts all of two minutes, with us dropping all the guards. Luckily, no one on our side was hit. We advance down the hall, checking doors on our way.

Within a few minutes, the second explosion hits. I have to give them credit, the Chipmunks sure know their explosives. The blast is controlled and only takes out its intended area. I can hear shouting up ahead. Kip motions for us to stop at a door at the end of the hallway.

"Grenade," he whispers back to us. We duck and take cover as he opens the door just slightly and tosses his grenade. It goes off and we immediately move through the doors. There are two guards on the ground near the door. We head towards the medical wing. On our way there, we find Jax laying on the ground.

I immediately run over to him and check for a pulse. He is still alive, just knocked out. One of the guys on our team is our acting medic and he checks him out. He has some blood on his temple.

"Blow to the head," the medic says. "I'll stay with him."

Kip nods and motions for us to move forward. I take one last glance at Jax and move on with my team. We enter the main hallway of the medical ward next. There are several guards lining the hallway. It makes me think that Cassidy is in one of these rooms.

"Clear the hall," Kip shouts, and we all advance.

There are a lot of bullets exchanged between us and them. They are trained, that much is true, but not well. I am reminded of Storm Troopers from Star Wars. They fire a lot of shots but not many hit their marks. We drop them quickly, checking rooms as we move along.

"Coop, over here," Kip says, calling me to the room he was checking.

I jog over and take a look inside. There is a lot of equipment in the room. I see everything from heart monitors to blood tubes and syringes. There is an IV pole standing with a bag that is actively dripping onto the floor. Someone left here in a hurry, and I would bet my ass it was Anderson with Cassidy. I hear a small moan and turn to find a young girl laying on the floor behind the door.

I rush over to her and gently turn her so I can see her face. She blinks her eyes rapidly, waking up from being knocked out.

"Don't worry, we won't hurt you. We are United States Marines, and we are here to rescue you," I explain, trying not to frighten her being that we are all in combat gear carrying guns.

"You have to hurry! He took her. He took her and she needs help," she fires off quickly.

"Who, honey? Who took who, where?" I ask.

"Dr. Anderson. He took Cassidy," she says, and my heart rate immediately picks up at the sound of her name.

"Where did he take her?" I fire back at her, trying not to sound angry, but I am. What if he's gone? What if he got out of the building somehow?

She looks at me, for what is probably only a second, but feels like so much longer. "You're Cooper. Aren't you?"

I am shocked for a second but quickly recover. "Who are you?"

"I'm Shelby. I met Cassidy the last time she was here and helped take care of her this time. You're all she talks about," she explains with a small smile.

I hold my hand out to her. "Hi, Shelby. I've heard a lot about you, too. Yes, I'm Cooper," I say, shaking her hand. "Shelby, I need to know where he went. I have to find her."

She shakes her head. "I don't know for sure, but I would guess he went down to the research rooms in the basement."

I nod. "Austin!" I shout and he comes running over. I explain who Shelby is quickly. "She thinks that Anderson probably took her to the basement. Let's go."

He runs over to tell Kip. I help Shelby up and take her over to sit down in one of the chairs in the room. "Shelby, stay here. We will come back for you after we find Cassidy. I promise we will come back."

She nods. "Please find her. She doesn't have much time left."

This stops me dead in my tracks. "What do you mean?"

A tear rolls down her cheek. "She is not in good shape, Cooper. I don't know how much more of his experimenting she can take."

"Kip!" I shout. Let's roll," I shout, moving towards the door. "I'll find her, Shelby. I will."

We hit the hallway running towards the door marked stairs. Once we open the door, we are immediately fired on by the guards in the stairwell. We must be going the right way because there are more guards in this stairwell than we have seen the whole time. We are in such close quarters, we end up going hand-to-hand with several of them, trying to get them out of our way. Kip takes a knife to the arm, and I jump in to help him. The guy is sloppy with his knife skills, but he is a big fucker. If there's one thing I learned, it's that the bigger they are, the slower they are. I push Kip to the side and dive at the fucker's legs to take him down. We end up going down a flight of stairs, toppling over each other on our way down. I land on top of him and immediately stab him in the heart with my knife. Austin flies down the stairs to check on me.

"I'm good. Keep moving," I say, rolling to my feet.

There is shouting down the stairs and we take off. When we get to the bottom, the door is locked from the other side.

"Fuck," Kip shouts. "How are we going to get through? That's a solid steel door, no way to knock it down."

I look to my left and see a fire box with an axe in it. I smash the glass and grab the axe. "Move," I shout, and everyone jumps out of the way. I hack at the door handle until it comes off. Once that is out of the way, Austin pulls the door open. Before he even gets the door open, he is shot in the leg. He drops to the ground, crying out. I pull him back into the stairwell and fall to his side.

"Aus. Talk to me, buddy."

"It went through. It's not too bad. Go get my sister, Coop. Don't stop until you have her," he growls as Kip wraps a bandage around his leg.

The rest of us gather quickly by the door, ready to surge forward.

"Bag out," I call, pulling the pin on a grenade. I open the door slightly and toss it through. Within a few seconds, it goes off and there is shouting on the other side. We take the opportunity to rush forward. The remaining guards in the hall run at us.

I take the biggest guy in front, hitting him immediately in the jaw. I am running on anger and fear right now. Fear from what Shelby told me. I swear to all that is holy that if she doesn't make it... I can't even finish that sentence.

The guy comes back at me with a shot to the side of my head. My ears ring for a second before I shake my head and go right back at him. We trade blow after blow, equally matched in size and speed. He pulls his knife and tries to swipe at my middle. I avoid it and swipe my leg out to drop him to the ground. I pounce on him as soon as he goes down. We roll around, fighting for the upper hand. I finally get him with a hit to the head which knocks him out cold.

In the time that it took for us to have our little fight, my team took out the rest of the guards. There are a lot of doors to check in this hall. Kip motions for silence and we all stand still. I don't hear anything. It's eerily quiet.

He motions for us to split up, half on one side, half on the other. We check doors as we make our way down the hall. I get to the third one on my side and motion to my guys that I am going in. I pull open the door and jump inside with my gun at the ready. The first thing I see, is Anderson, standing behind several guards. The next thing I see, is a body lying in the corner of the room.

Cassidy.

And that's when all hell breaks loose.

Chapter 18
Victory... or Is It Defeat
Cooper

The moment I see Cassidy in a pile on the floor, my vision goes red. I charge Anderson. I dive at him, but just before I hit him, I am hit hard from the side. One of his guards takes me down and we land hard on the floor. We roll over each other, grappling for the upper hand. I land a blow to his head, but he counters with one to my jaw. We trade hits back and forth until I finally knock him out with an elbow to the nose. He goes down hard.

I look around and see several of our men in their own fights with the rest of the guards. Anderson is standing in front of Cassidy like he is guarding her. He is looking around frantically. He has the look of someone who knows he has lost. I jump to my feet and take a step toward him.

"Stay there! Or I'll kill her," he warns me, aiming a gun at her head. I stop, not wanting to give him any incentive to do her any more harm. I know he won't kill her, otherwise, why would he have so many guards with him protecting her? He needs her.

"Don't. I stopped," I say, holding my hands up in front of me, trying to calm him. If there is one thing I've learned over my years in the Marines, it's that a rash person is not in their right mind. Anything can set them off.

"You can't have her," he growls at me. "I need her to finish my research." He takes a step closer to her. She hasn't moved, but I can just make out the rise and fall of her chest. She's alive, lucky for him.

The other men must have won their individual fights because it has grown eerily quiet in the room. I chance a look around and see all of Anderson's guards on the floor, and my men inching closer to Anderson. I hold my hand up to halt their progression.

Anderson has literally backed himself into a corner. He has nowhere to run, and no way out, which makes him very dangerous. I look to my left and nod at Kip just slightly. I can tell that he knows what I mean as he starts to shift slightly to his left. He is the closest to the wall. If I can get Anderson to keep his attention on me, Kip might be able to take him down. I start to shift slightly to the right, farther away from Kip. Anderson spots my movement and points his gun at me.

"I said, stop!" he shouts at me. "Do you think I am stupid, boy? I know exactly what you are doing, and it won't work. Miss Daniels is my property. She was turned into my facility therefore, she belongs to the government," he snaps at me.

His property? She belongs to the government? I growl, loudly.

"Ah. I see. You're the one she moans about in her sleep. Cooper, is it? So, I guess that makes you the father, then."

I stop moving. Father? Cassidy is pregnant.

I must smile slightly because he smiles sardonically. "Oh, I'm sorry. Maybe you didn't hear the news. Cassidy lost the baby. Well, not so much lost as I took it from her," he taunts me, which is the wrong thing to do.

I roar, loudly. The next few seconds happen in slow motion. I dive at Anderson. He raises his gun and fires, just as Kip takes him down from the side. I feel a searing pain in my left arm, but it doesn't stop me. I land on top of Kip and Anderson, fighting with Kip to get my hands around Anderson's throat.

"Coop! Coop! Stop! He's not worth it!" Kip shouts at me, but nothing is getting through. I keep fighting and fighting. I land a couple of blows to Anderson's face, hearing a crunch. I grin knowing that I broke his nose. A couple of the men drag me off him before I can do any more damage. I shrug out of their hold and fix my clothes.

I got so caught up in getting to Anderson that I almost forgot about Cassidy.

"Cass," I say, dropping to the floor at her side. When I roll her over so I can see her face, I gasp. Her face is swollen and bruised, and her nose is obviously broken. Her lips are cracked and dry. There is blood caked in her hair. She has lost a lot of weight. She is skin and bones. I look over her body and notice that her right arm looks like it has been melted and her hand is swollen, all her fingers are broken. The bottom half of her is covered in blood, and I can only assume it is from her losing the baby. "Oh, my sweet Cassidy," I say pulling her gently into my arms. I kiss her head as I rock us back and forth.

I wasn't sure I would get to hold her again, and now that I have her in my arms, I am at a loss. Part of me is overjoyed that she is still alive, but the other part is horrified by the condition that she is in. I know that she needs medical attention, but I just can't bring myself to move yet. She is finally, *finally*, back in my arms and I am whole again.

She hasn't so much as made a sound since we have been in here. I look over at Anderson. "What did you do to her?" I growl at him.

He laughs, and Kip quickly punches him in the face, which shuts him up.

"What. Did you. Do. To her," I say slowly, enunciating every word.

He rubs his jaw where Kip punched him. He has blood pouring from his nose where I broke it, his right eye is swollen shut, and I can see that I knocked one of his front teeth out. "I had to test my serums on somebody. And with her blood, I knew she could handle it. You're lucky I didn't kill her," he has the gall to say, and Kip backhands him across the face.

"Let's go, Coop. We have to get Cassidy medical attention," Kip says, tugging Anderson to his feet. They secure him with zip ties and thankfully gag him, and drag him out of the room, leaving me alone with Cassidy.

I hold her close, breathing her in. She is breathing, but it is shallow. "I promise you will be ok, Cass. I'm here now. I'm so sorry. I love you, baby," I say into her hair.

Her eyes flutter slightly, and she moans. "Cooper," she whispers quietly.

I choke back a sob. "Yeah, baby. I'm here and I'm never letting you go."

"Cooper," she says again as her eyes close, and then she's out again.

I stand with her in my arms and carry her from the room. When we get to the end of the hallway, Austin is leaning against the wall.

"Cassidy!" he shouts, trying to limp over to me.

I stop at his side, and he gasps. "What the fuck did they do to her? Cassidy, honey, I'm so sorry," he says, leaning down and touching his forehead to hers.

"Let's go," I say. "We have to get her back as soon as possible." I turn to look at one of our guys. "Hey, Johnson. There is a young girl back in the medical ward. Her name is Shelby. She needs to come back with us. Can you find her and bring her in your vehicle?"

He nods and takes off in that direction. I know that the men have a lot of work to do to finish up this mission. Gathering the survivors, tending to the wounded, and collecting the evidence. I don't worry about any of that right now. My only concern is Cassidy.

We make our way out of the facility and back to the vehicles. I slide into the back of one of the Jeeps with Cassidy in my arms. I am not letting her go. No one will take her from me again. I grab a blanket from the back and wrap her in it. She is so cold; her skin is like ice. Austin slides into the front seat while Kip drives. We don't wait for everyone else as we take off toward home. Everyone is silent for a while, trying to absorb everything that just happened. I know she is in my arms, but I just can't wrap my head around everything that he did to her. Eventually, Austin looks back at Cassidy. I know he saw her briefly at the prison, but I'm sure he wasn't able to take it all in.

"My God, Coop. She is skin and bones. Her face... her hand." He puts his hand up and covers his mouth in disbelief.

Austin grabs a cloth from his bag and wets it. He hands it to me. "Clean her up, man. I can't handle seeing her like this."

"Thanks," I say, grabbing the cloth. I gently clean her face. Her hair is stringy, greasy, like it hasn't been washed in days. Her broken nose is recent, or at least it looks like it is. I try not to touch her right arm. I have no idea what happened to it, but it is mangled, and will definitely require surgery to repair it.

"Austin. They can fix her, right? The doctors at the base... they can make her better," I plead, needing someone to reassure me.

"She'll be fine, Coop," Kip says. "The General has the best doctors on staff. They will take good care of her."

I lean down and kiss her forehead. She stirs again, her eyes fluttering.

"Cooper," she moans.

"I'm here, baby. I'm here. Austin's here, too. We're going to get you better, baby. I promise. I'm not leaving you," I say, holding her tighter.

We make the rest of the drive, in silence. I spend the time watching her breathe, just looking at her. It's only been a couple of weeks since she was taken, but it feels like a lifetime. I keep leaning down and whispering to her that I am here, that I love her. I kiss her and touch her. I think about how we actually took down the prison, and that we were able to capture Anderson. But I don't feel like we can call this a victory, not with what they did to Cassidy. I knew he would hurt her, torture her. But I never thought, in a million years, that he would come this close to killing her.

I plan to ask the General for some time alone with Anderson. I want to be there when they question him. I need to be there. Because when the time comes, I will be the one to end his life.

Chapter 19
Anger
Cooper

When we finally make it back to base, there is a team of doctors and nurses, waiting for our arrival. We called ahead and let them know the situation so they would be ready for Cassidy. I get out of the Jeep and am immediately rushed by everyone. Someone tries to pull her out of my arms, and I growl.

"Coop, you have to let them have her. They have to help her," Austin pleads with me.

I look at them and down at Cassidy. I know I have to hand her over, but I'm just not ready to let her go. I just got her back.

"Staff Sergeant Matthews," another voice says.

The General walks up and stops short when he sees Cassidy. His face is hard, and angry. "Let them have her son," he tells me.

I nod, knowing that he's right.

I lay her gently on the gurney that they brought for her. I lean down and kiss her forehead. "I'll be right here, Cassidy. I'm not leaving. I promise. I'll be right here when you wake up, baby. I love you," I tell her, caressing her cheek.

I stand up and nod at them. They quickly wheel her away. I just stand there and watch them walk away with my heart. Austin comes to stand beside me. He places his hand on my shoulder. We don't say anything because we don't have to. We are both feeling the same thing.

I feel someone come up behind us and know who it is without looking.

"Boys, I am so sorry. I didn't think it would be this bad. None of us thought he was capable of this kind of behavior," the General says.

I turn around and look at him. In this moment, I am not a Marine looking at a commanding officer. I am a man, looking at another man, who is responsible for what happened to Cassidy.

"Sir, I have the utmost respect for you and all you have done for this cause. But right now, I can't even stand the sight of you. You... you did this to her. You made her think she had to go back there. You asked her to do this and look where it got her. She is almost dead, sir. What would you do if that was your wife, your daughter? I... I just..." I stop, not sure I have anything else to say to him.

"Cooper, I understand what you are feeling..." he starts, but I cut him off. "You have no idea what I am going through! No clue! You don't understand shit! I blame you, sir. If she... if she dies. If something happens to her, I don't care what happens to me. I will put a bullet between Anderson's eyes," I shout, and then storm away.

I head into the hospital and stop at the front desk. "Where did they take Cassidy Daniels?" I ask the woman behind the desk.

She tells me to follow her, and I do. We head down a hallway and into the last room. I see Cassidy on a bed, hooked up to all kinds of tubes and wires. One of the doctors turns and sees me in the door.

"Hi, Staff Sergeant," he says with a small smile. He walks over and offers me his hand. "I'm Dr. Tom Stevens. I'll be taking care of Cassidy."

"Hello, Dr. Stevens. I am Staff Sergeant Cooper Matthews. I am Cassidy's boy... fiancé." I almost said boyfriend, but we are well beyond that. The second she is able I will marry her. "Please tell me she is going to be ok."

"I'm not going to lie. She is in pretty bad shape. We have her on fluids and supplements to get her stable. She is severely emaciated and malnourished. Just by looking at her, I couldn't even tell you the last time that she has eaten. She is dehydrated. She needs surgery to fix her nose and her hand. Her arm is terribly infected from whatever they did to her. We have to get her hydrated and stronger before we can even consider surgery," he explains. He looks at me with a strange expression.

"Sir, the x-rays of her hand – I've never seen anything like it. Her fingers were broken deliberately. Her hand has several broken bones. I can only hope that the surgery will be able to repair it. There is the possibility that she won't have full function of that hand ever again."

I make my way over and pick up her good hand. I look back over at the doctor. "It doesn't matter, doc. I will take care of her for the rest of her life, no matter what she needs. Just do everything you can for her. I don't want her in any more pain."

"We already started pain medication," he tells me.

I pull up a chair and sit down next to her, holding her hand in both of mine. I notice the doctor hasn't left so I look at him, raising my eyebrows.

"Is there something else, doc?"

He clears his throat. "Yes, there is. All those things that I told you are not the worst of my concerns. I don't know what he did to her. I heard that he gave her some type of injections, but I have no idea what was in them." He pauses, seeming to struggle with his words. "The other thing is her head. She is in a coma of sorts right now. Her mind needs time to heal. There is evidence of several strong blows to the head, and she definitely has a concussion. I can't guarantee that she will wake up, no matter what we do," he finishes, and my heart drops.

"She said my name a few times since we found her. Isn't that a good sign?" I ask.

"I wish I could say. We will do everything we can and hope for the best," he tells me.

"Doc. What about the baby? She was," I start, but have to stop to catch the sob. "She was pregnant but lost the baby."

He looks down at the floor. "I know. She is bleeding heavily, but that is the body recovering from the loss. We will monitor that as well."

I thank him and he leaves the room quietly, leaving me alone with Cassidy.

I sit there, simply holding her hand. I watch the heart monitor, her breathing.

"Cassidy, I am so, so sorry, baby. I feel like this is my fault. I never should have left you. I should have been there to protect you."

Part of me is waiting for her to respond, to tell me that I am being ridiculous. But I know that's not going to happen. I think about what the doctor said that she might not wake up. I refuse to believe that. Cassidy will wake up, she has to. Because I don't know what I will do otherwise.

A nurse comes in at one point to take a look at the wound on my arm from when Anderson shot at me. Thankfully, the bullet just grazed me. She cleans my arm and applies a bandage quickly, and then leaves.

There is a soft knock at the door and Austin comes in. He doesn't make it two steps and he is crying. I get up and move to her other side so that Austin can sit and hold her good hand.

"What did the doc say?" he asks, pushing some of her hair behind her ear.

I tell him everything that the doctor told me, including the little fact that he is not sure she is going to wake up.

"I'll kill him," he growls

"When are they questioning him?" I ask, knowing Austin stayed behind to talk to the General.

"In about an hour. The General wants him to sit for a bit and worry about what is going to happen," he explains.

"Am I in trouble?" I ask, not really caring.

He laughs. "Well, he wasn't exactly thrilled with you, but he understands where you are coming from. He said if it was his wife or daughter, he would feel the same way."

"How could you even stand to talk to him, Aus? This happened because of him," I say, reaching out and touching Cassidy's cheek, needing the connection.

"It wasn't his fault, Cooper. Yeah, he wanted her to go back to get information. But she was taken. Those men took her there, but this is because of Anderson. He did this to her. Don't hold this against the General."

I just grunt, not willing to agree at this point. "Is he going to let me be there for the questioning?"

"Yeah, we both are expected there."

We sit there in silence for a while, just staring at her, willing her to get better. She is already looking a little less pale since they started the fluids. She still has a long road ahead and I intend to be here every step of the way. I don't care if she can't use her hand, I don't care if her nose is a little crooked or if her skin is scarred. She is my life.

A little while later, Austin breaks the silence. "Coop, we have to go if we are going to make it to the questioning."

"I don't know if I can leave her, man. I just can't," I say, feeling anxious about leaving her at all, let alone by herself.

"I can sit with her," a small voice says from the doorway.

We both turn to see her friend Shelby standing there. She looks a lot better from when we found her in the prison. You can tell that she has showered. She is in a fresh pair of cotton pants and long sleeve shirt. Her hair is clean and dry, laying softly down her back. She has some bruising on her face, but overall, looks ok.

"Shelby, how are you?" I ask.

"I'm doing ok. Well, as good as can be expected. It still doesn't feel real, that I am free and safe. That's definitely going to take some getting used to," she explains with a slight laugh.

"Well, you are most definitely safe. But you take whatever time you need to heal," Austin says.

She makes her way over to Cassidy's sleeping form and touches her leg. "I'm so sorry that this happened to her," she whispers.

"Hey. You have nothing to apologize about. This is not your fault. If anything, we owe you for everything you did for her there," I say.

"I wasn't allowed to do much, but I tried. I'm just glad I was with her... when she lost the baby. At least she wasn't alone," she says with a tear running down her face.

I feel a sharp pain in my chest. "So, she knew she was pregnant?"

She nods. "But not until they told her. She called him her little bean. She was so happy about it. She was happy to have a piece of you with her, no matter how small."

"Bean," I say with a small smile. Only Cassidy would call a baby that. "It was a boy?"

"She didn't know for sure, but she always called it a boy. She talked about how she hoped he looked like you. She said it was the only thing keeping her going. That if she was going to die, at least she had a piece of you with her."

My heart broke right that very second. She was hoping for a boy that looked like me. She is amazing. That even when she thought she was going to die she was thinking of me.

"Shelby, can you sit with her for a little while? Austin and I have something we have to take care of, and I don't want her alone," I say. "I don't want to leave her but knowing that you're here will make it a little easier."

She nods. "Of course. I would love to sit with her."

I lean down and kiss Cassidy on the forehead. "I'll be back soon, baby. I love you."

Chapter 20
Interrogations
Cooper

Austin and I walk into the building where they are keeping Anderson. The first person I see is the General. Austin stops to talk to someone, but I make my way over to him.

"General," I say, saluting him. "I want to apologize for my behavior earlier. While I may not completely agree with Austin that you are not at fault, I had no right to act that way. I respect you and everything that you have done."

He smiles. "It's ok. I deserved that and more. I want you to know, Cooper, that if I had known exactly what he was doing, I would have never asked that of her. I would never willingly put anyone in that position."

"I know, sir. But we have more pressing matters to deal with right now," I say, looking towards the room that Anderson is in.

"That we do, son."

We make our way over to the guards who immediately salute the General. "Let us in, boys." Austin turns to go into the observation room. I don't think he trusts himself near Anderson right now. I don't really trust myself, but I need to be in there.

Right before they open the door, he turns and looks me in the eyes. "Cooper, I am trusting you here. You are not to kill him, under any circumstance. We need information that only he can provide. I will sideline you if I have to, but I am giving you the benefit of the doubt here."

"I understand, sir."

He nods and opens the door. We enter the room and find another two soldiers standing guard.

"Leave," the General says firmly, and they quickly exit the room, leaving us alone with Anderson.

He looks worried. He is handcuffed to the table. They changed him into a jumpsuit. I smile when I see the bruising around his eyes and his crooked nose. Someone has cleaned up the blood, but you can clearly see that I did some damage.

"Ah, the boyfriend. Tell me, Cooper, how is dear Cassidy doing?" he asks while smiling.

I fight the urge to dive over the table and strangle him. I remember, however, what the General said. That he would sideline me, and I need to be here. I need to know the reason he did all those things to Cassidy.

"She is doing just fine. She will be back to normal in no time," I say, trying to gain the upper hand.

"Now, now, soldier. It is not nice to lie," he says smugly. I take a step towards him, ready to punch him, when the General grabs my arm.

"Enough!" the General barks. "We need information, and you are going to provide it. If you don't, I will unleash Staff Sergeant Matthews."

Anderson gulps but tries to cover it up with a smile. "Well, then General. Ask away." He is trying to remain cocky, but I just smile to myself when I see his missing tooth every time he smiles. Knowing that I did that, well, let's just say it's satisfying.

"Who were you working for?" the General wastes no time getting down to business.

"Sorry, General. That's classified. You should know all about that," Anderson sneers.

"Well, now, I guess I should tell you that I already know it was Vice President Thompson. I was only giving you the chance to be honest with us."

Anderson looks shocked. "There is no way you can prove that!"

"Well, I hate to tell you this, but you're wrong again. You let that little piece of information slip to Cassidy, who then reported it to my man on the inside, who then reported it directly to me," General McConnell says.

Anderson scowls at that admission. "You planted her there, didn't you?"

"No. She was legitimately picked up by those scavengers and turned into your facility. I just had a man on the inside getting information from her. Everything that you told Cassidy, made its way back to me."

"Who was it!" he shouts, sitting up straight in his chair, and slamming his fist on the table.

"Now, now, Dr. Anderson. I am the one asking the questions here," the General warns.

He slumps back down, mumbling under his breath about finding out who it was and killing them. He is staring daggers at the General right now. If looks could kill and all that.

"Tell me what the Vice President wanted you to do," the General says.

"Well, if you had a man on the inside, I'm sure you already know," Anderson says to taunt the General.

"Cooper," the General says, allowing me the first hit.

I cross the room in three strides and punch Anderson in the face, and he howls in pain. I hear the crunch of his nose. I already broke it at the facility, but I just did some more damage, and that makes me smile. I take a step back and just stare down at him. The General goes over to the table and takes the seat across from Anderson. I stand next to Anderson with my arms crossed, hoping to intimidate him. All I need is another nod from General.

"We can do this the easy way or the hard way. It's completely up to you, doctor," the General tells him, laying his hands in front of him on the table.

"I vote for the hard way," I growl.

Anderson casts a sideways glance at me. He knows he is beaten, no pun intended. He doesn't want to give up the information, but he has no choice. I don't think anyone is prepared for what he tells us, though, as he begins to tell his story.

"Back in the beginning, I was doing research for President Murphy. I was looking into the possibility of creating a vaccine for Alzheimer's Disease. A complete waste of my time and genius if you ask me. Then the first event happened, and everyone panicked. After the second wave hit, I got a call from Dan, er, Vice President Thompson, about working for him on a new project. He initially wanted me to just figure out what it was that happened. He kept calling it "the virus", no matter how many times I told him that I couldn't prove it was a virus. It really is a shame how utterly stupid our leaders are, and how little they know." He stops and takes a drink of water from the cup in front of him. "Now, where was I? Oh yes, my new assignment. Dan kept pushing me to figure out what caused the events, while President Murphy was too busy worrying about what to do with all the unrest and riots throughout the country. I spent the next few weeks doing basic research on the bodies that were brought to me in my lab. I did everything I could to determine what killed everyone but kept hitting dead ends. I approached Dan and told him that what I really needed were live subjects. If I could get my hands on surviving females, I would have a better chance of figuring it out. That's when he started his task force. He began emptying out prisons across the country to create research facilities for my team. I was allowed to choose my own team of doctors and researchers, and of course, I chose the best of the best. Dan offered all of them generous stipends for helping in his cause. The only stipulation that we were given is that we had to... well, let's just say we had to encourage the surviving female subjects to reproduce. He decided that in order to justify our research, we had to make it look like we were only out to create more life, more females. He passed our research off to the President by telling him that we were only taking samples to determine who had the best chance of producing female offspring. And the President fell for it, hook, line, and sinker. And so, our research began. I hired teams of men to go out and collect females for my research. The men that I found had less than stellar morals and were not afraid to go above and beyond. They were rewarded handsomely for their help. All I had to do was pay one group of men and word spread like wildfire. Within a month, all facilities were up and running."

Anderson looks smug telling his story, almost like he is proud of what he's done. It really bothered me that he referred to the women that he experimented on as "samples." As if their lives didn't matter.

"And did it occur to you at any point in time that what you were doing was unethical?" I ask.

"Unethical? No. Not for one second. I was helping with repopulation all while investigating what happened. I was doing nothing wrong," he says, again smug.

I slam my hands down on the table, making him jump. "Nothing wrong! You paraded women in front of a room full of men, naked! You made those men battle to the death for the chance to essentially rape her. You tortured and beat said women for your own pleasure! How can you sit there and say that you did nothing wrong?" I scream at him.

"Cooper, stand down," the General warns me.

"I will not stand down! He experimented on Cassidy to the point where she is barely hanging onto life. He murdered my unborn child! He damn near killed the woman I love. How can you tell me to stand down?"

The General allows me my little rant but tells me with a look that I am close to being kicked out of the room. I take a step back and calm myself. I need to be here.

"Did your research produce any results?" the General asks.

"Oh, there were results. Just not what he was looking for. I tested quite a few serums on dear Miss Daniels, but they didn't have the intended results. I did succeed in causing some distress, though," Anderson says, chuckling, which earns him a backhand across the face.

"That's a warning!" I growl. "Bring up Cassidy again, say her name, one more time, and it will be the last thing you do."

He rubs his face, where I hit him, glaring at me. "At ease, soldier. What I meant was, the serums that I produced were intended to kill, not cause pain or physical damage. The fact that Miss Daniels is still alive proves that there is something in her blood that makes her resistant, immune almost. Most of those serums would have killed any normal human. But she is special."

I take an involuntary step toward him but catch myself. The General is scribbling things down in a notebook. I know that he is on a mission, trying to figure out how to stop this whole thing.

"So, why is the Vice President so worried about recreating this thing?" he asks, and that's the big question.

"Well, I'm sure you know the answer to that as well. But I will humor you and answer. You are an educated man, obviously. You have worked your way up the chain of command in the Army. You know things that most people don't. You must know that the world that we live in is all about power. Not too long ago, the great leaders of this world were battling over the world's nuclear weapons. Whoever had the most, was deemed the most powerful. Well, the Vice President decided that if he were to have his hands on whatever this was that killed our women, he would be the most powerful man in the world. If I could create a serum that could kill not only any woman, but any man, and make it so that it could kill millions at a time, well... the value of that speaks for itself."

I am taken aback by that statement. What kind of a person do you have to be? How evil does your mind have to be to want to possess such a product? To want to be able to kill millions at a time is unfathomable. It's just insane. War is an unfortunate byproduct of human nature. I, myself, have been in active combat and know how it feels to kill. I live with that every day. But I can't stand here and say that anything condones the use of a weapon of mass destruction. I fight other soldiers, others like me. I have never taken an innocent life.

"Do you have documentation, proof that you were working under his orders?"

He laughs. "Of course, I do. I am a big believer in covering my ass. I have emails and texts from him from the very beginning."

Anderson and the General talk about getting copies of those emails and texts for a few minutes. I take to time to think about what he said. He developed a bunch of serums and tested them on Cassidy? What her poor little body went through. It's too hard to think about.

I interrupt them. "You said you tested your serums on Cassidy. What will they do to her?"

The General looks at me sympathetically. He then turns to Anderson. "Answer the question."

Anderson chuckles. "Well, the damage has already been done. Let me see if I can remember all the side effects that she had from my work. There was blindness, severe pain, the loss of the baby, the chemical burns," he starts ticking them off, one by one, counting them on his fingers.

"Stop!" I shout, not able to listen to any more of it. "Will she wake up?"

"Well, it really depends on how much damage I have done internally. The last I checked, her kidneys were shutting down and her liver wasn't far behind. But that was a few days ago. I was ready to take more blood but then you and you merry little men invaded my facility."

I have had enough. I jump on him and start wailing away. I think I am yelling as well, but I really don't know. There is a lot of noise. Austin and several men burst through the door and try to pull me off him. I grab my sidearm and point it directly at his temple. This halts everything immediately. The men who are holding me take a step back. I see the General take a step closer. Austin, who is standing right next to me, pulls his gun out as well.

"Cooper. Austin," he says as a warning. "Think about what you are doing."

"I am thinking. I am thinking that this asshole needs to die," I say, a tear running down my cheek. I'm not embarrassed at all about crying in front of anyone. "What this man did to Cassidy is unforgivable."

"I agree, wholeheartedly. But you cannot kill him. He needs to stand trial for his crimes. He will spend the rest of his life in prison," the General says.

I think about that for a second. If he stands trial, there is no way he would not be found guilty. He would spend his life, rotting away in a prison. I look at Austin and nod.

We both lower our weapons, and Anderson drops to the ground, moaning in pain. He is bleeding in several places.

"Cooper," the General says to get my attention. "Go back to Cassidy. She needs you right now."

That's all I need to hear.

Chapter 21
Waiting
Cooper

It's been a couple of weeks since we've been back at base. Cassidy's physical wounds are healing, but she still hasn't woken up. They did an extensive workup on her and determined that yes, her kidneys were failing. They are pumping her full of fluids to try and flush her system of any of the toxins. They are supposed to take more blood today to see if there has been any improvement. If there is, they will schedule her for surgery to repair her hand. They decided that her nose will heal on its own. It is slightly crooked now, but she is still the most beautiful woman I have ever seen.

I haven't left her side. Austin keeps trying to get me to leave, to get some rest, but I just can't bring myself to walk out of this room. He keeps bringing me clothes and I shower quickly and change in the adjoining bathroom. The staff here keeps me fed. Austin and Shelby come in every day to sit with her for a while. Shelby has taken to reading to Cassidy. She said during their time together at the facility, she learned that Cassidy loves the classics. Right now, she is sitting next to her bed, reading her Little Women.

Even when they are here, I can't bring myself to leave. I have this fear that if I leave, I will miss her waking up. And I want my face to be the first thing that she sees when she wakes up.

"Knock, knock," one of the nurses, Michelle, sings as she walks into the room. "How's our patient today?"

"She is looking a little better today. Her face has more color," I say, brushing some of the hair out of her face.

"I'm here to take some blood. Is that ok?" she asks.

"Of course," I tell her.

Shelby stands. "I'm going to head out, Cooper. Do you need anything?"

I look down at Cassidy. "No. I'm good. Everything I need is right here."

Michelle takes the blood and changes the fluid bag. She adds some medication to the bag and tells me that she will be back shortly to give her the pain medication. They have been giving her pain medication just in case she wakes up. They don't want her pain to be the thing that brings her out of this.

I sit down next to the bed and take her good hand. I kiss the back of it and hold it close to me.

"Cassidy. Baby? Can you hear me?" I start. I talk to her a lot. They tell me that there is a good possibility that she can hear me. "I'm here. I'm right by your side and I'm not leaving. You take whatever time you need to heal. I'll take care of you from this side."

A little while later, there is another knock on the door. Dr. Stevens walks in. He has overseen Cassidy's care since she was admitted.

"Hi, Staff Sergeant."

"Doc, I have told you before, call me Cooper."

He chuckles. "Sorry, Cooper. I didn't want to disrespect you," he says with a smile. "Well, I have some good news. Her kidney values are getting close to normal. They are still slightly elevated, but I think we are in a good place to do surgery now. I don't want to put it off any longer for fear that we won't be able to correct the damage that's been done."

I nod. "Of course. Whatever you need to do, doc. When can you do it?"

"I am going to do it first thing tomorrow. I have the best hand specialist on the east coast coming in tonight. His name is Shawn Watson, from the University of Pennsylvania. He's been doing this for thirty years. If anyone can fix her hand, it's him."

I sigh a sigh of relief. Finally, something is going in her favor. "That's great news. Great news, doc. Thank you."

"You can thank me when she walks out of this hospital, Cooper," he says while writing something on his clipboard. "We'll be in to get her in the morning."

As he is leaving, Austin comes in and I fill him in on the good news.

"Well, that's great. Hopefully, this guy will be able to repair all the damage. It still makes me cringe to think that she was awake when they did that to her. I wish we would have pulled the trigger on Anderson," Austin says angrily.

"Me, too. But the more I think about it, the more I think he should rot away in some prison for the rest of his life. Maybe we can convince the General to give him some of the serums that he gave Cassidy."

"That's a fine idea, now that you say it," he says.

We shoot the shit for a while. He fills me in on what's been going on. They issued a warrant for Vice President Thompson, but he has gone into hiding. President Murphy has ordered all the other facilities to close. He created a task force that is going to each one and arresting any of those who oppose. A few of Anderson's top researchers have also been arrested. They didn't know who he was working for, but they were helping Anderson develop the serums that they knew would be tested on Cassidy.

We know that Anderson wanted Cassidy because she seemed to be immune, but we will never know the full extent of his obsession with her. There have been many other women who have similar blood traits to Cassidy, and he knew about them but didn't care. He only wanted Cassidy. Maybe they will give me some time with him, and I can beat it out of him.

Society in general is slowly returning to as close to normal as possible. People are beginning to clean up their homes and neighborhoods. The President has created memorials in each state dedicated to those that were lost. Not only the women but those like

Cassidy's father who were killed protecting their loved ones. No one knows how long it will take to build up the population of females. We have heard that doctors are researching ways to ensure that pregnancies result in female offspring. If that doesn't work, it will just have to happen naturally.

No one has been able to figure out what it was that actually happened. They have spent a lot of time and money trying to but to no avail. There are many now, that agree with the theory that it was divine intervention. That this was a punishment from above. I, myself, don't believe that theory. I don't know that we will ever know what happened. The scary thing is that without knowing, we have no way to prevent it from happening again.

Austin leaves for the night, and I climb into bed with Cassidy. Right after she got here, and they realized I wouldn't be leaving, they brought in one of those double maternity beds for me to sleep in with Cassidy. I lay down next to her, careful not to jostle all the tubes and wires coming out of her. I lay as close to her as possible, holding her good hand.

"Sleep well, my love. I'll be here when you wake," I whisper, kissing her on the forehead.

Chapter 22
Healing
Cooper

Her surgery was a success. Dr. Watson was able to repair the fractures in Cassidy's hand and fingers, and she should make a full recovery. It will take a lot of physical therapy, but she will be fine. Now the only thing left is for her to wake up. It has been several weeks and there is still no sign of her waking. I told her to take as much time as she needs, and I meant it. I can only imagine the torture that she went through with everything. They keep telling me to be prepared, that she may not be the same when she wakes up after everything that she went through. But I know that no matter what, I will take care of her. I intend to marry her as soon as she is able. I have made arrangements for some of the men to go to my cabin and clean it up. It's been so long since I have been there that I know it is in bad shape. I want to make sure that it is ready for us when she is able to go. That is where we will start our lives together.

It is the middle of the afternoon, a few days after her surgery, and I am lying in bed with her, playing with her hair. I have been bathing her every day, with the help of the nurses. I wanted to be the one to take care of her. I am holding her good hand when I feel her fingers twitch. It is a very slight movement, but I know I felt it.

"Cass," I say hopefully.

Her fingers twitch again. "Cassidy, baby? Open your eyes for me, love."

Her eyes flutter and her breathing picks up. I hit the call button for the nurse, and they immediately respond.

"Do you need something, Cooper?" Michelle asks.

"Something is happening," I say frantically jumping to my feet, and within a few seconds, Dr. Stevens, Michelle, and three other nurses come rushing into the room.

"She moved her fingers and her eyes fluttered," I say, moving out of the way so they can check her.

Dr. Stevens shines a light in her eyes while one of the nurses fiddles with the machines.

"Cassidy? Can you hear me?" Dr. Stevens asks.

Her fingers move again and this time, she makes a small sound. I rush to her side and grab her hand again. "Cassidy, I'm here. Open your eyes, baby."

I am leaning over her, staring at her, willing her to open her eyes. She opens her eyes just slightly. Her eyes are unfocused as she looks around the room.

"Coop?" she whispers, and I immediately start to cry.

"Yeah, baby. It's me. I'm here," I say between tears. She smiles, just slightly, but it's enough for me. I lean down and kiss her on the forehead.

"I know you've been waiting for this, Cooper, but let me take a look at her, really quickly, and then we will be out of your hair," Dr. Stevens says.

I take a step back, but don't let go of her hand. I can't. Dr. Stevens looks her over, testing her reflexes. She isn't able to move too much, but that's ok, we'll work on it. She doesn't say much, just yes and no when he asks her questions. I know I should call Austin, but I'm frozen to my spot, afraid I will miss something.

After a few minutes, the doc steps back and looks at me. He smiles a genuinely happy smile. "Cooper, she's all yours. Let her get some rest and call if you need anything at all," he says as he pats me on the back. He and the nurses make their way out of the room.

"Hey, doc," I call out, just before he leaves the room. "Thanks."

He smiles. "Anytime, Cooper."

"Can you call Austin for me?"

"Sure," he says, then leaves.

I crawl back onto the bed with her and kiss her head again. "You had me so scared, baby."

"Coop. I'm ok," she says, her voice scratchy. I offer her a sip of my water from lunch which she gladly takes. When she's finished, she smiles. "You look like hell, Coop."

I laugh and cry at the same time. "I didn't want to clean up and have the nurses hitting on me," I tease.

She laughs. She looks down at her body and sees her bandaged hand. She lifts it a little and winces.

"They did surgery a few days ago and fixed it. Should be good as new in a few weeks. You'll need to do some physical therapy, but that's it," I explain.

She looks confused for a second. "What happened, Coop? How did you get me out? What happened to Anderson?" She fires off questions, one after the other.

"Slow down, baby. We'll get to all of that. Just let me enjoy you a little longer before we start with the ugly stuff. Then suddenly, she starts to cry.

"What is it, Cass? Are you in pain, do you need something?"

She sniffles. "He killed our baby, Cooper. I lost him," she cries. I pull her close and hold her while she mourns the loss of our child. What do you say to that? There is nothing I can say that will make it any better.

"I'm so sorry, Cass. I'm so incredibly sorry. I wish I would have known. I wish I would have been there for you, with you."

She cries for a while until I hear her breathing even out. She's back asleep, and part of me is relieved. I wish I had the right words to make it better, to take away her pain. But I don't.

Austin comes tearing into the room and I quickly silence him with a wave of my hand. He sees her sleeping and comes over quietly.

"She woke up?" he whisper-shouts at me.

I nod. "Yeah. She was awake for about twenty minutes. She was talking and alert," I explain. "The doctor was very pleased."

"Then why don't you look happy?" he asks.

I lean down and kiss the top of her head. "Because one of the first things she asked about was the baby."

He puts his chin to his chest. "I'm sorry, man. So sorry. She shouldn't have had to go through any of what she did, especially losing your baby."

"I know. But we'll try again. If she wants a baby, we'll have as many as she wants. I will give her everything, Aus. She means that much to me."

He laughs. "I never thought I would see the day that you were completely whipped. But I'm glad it's with Cassidy. She couldn't find better."

I smile. We sit there talking for a bit when Cassidy stirs again. She blinks and opens her eyes.

"Hey, baby. How are you feeling?" I ask.

"Well, my eyebrows don't hurt, so there's that," she says.

"Hey, kid. Welcome back to the land of the living," Austin teases her.

She laughs. "Hi, Aus. Glad to be back."

He walks over and gives her a kiss on the forehead. I get up out of the bed. "Do you need anything, baby?" I ask her.

"Yeah. Can you help me sit up?"

Austin and I work together moving the bed and getting her up. I can't explain how good it is to see her awake and talking. The nurse comes in and checks her over. Once the three of us are alone again, she starts with the questions.

"Ok. Now tell me. What happened to Anderson? Did you take down the facility? Is Shelby ok?"

"Slow down, kid. We'll answer all your questions," Austin says.

We sit there for a while, explaining what happened while she was unconscious. We tell her about taking the facility down, about finding her and Anderson, about the standoff with Anderson, and his questioning. I explain about her surgery and recovery. Just as we finish talking, Shelby comes in, and I immediately feel guilty because we didn't call her to tell her that Cassidy is awake.

"Cassidy!" she yells, running over and throwing her arms around her.

"Easy, Shelby. I may be awake but I'm still fragile," Cassidy says with a giggle.

"Oh, I'm so sorry. I'm just so happy to see you awake!"

I look over at Shelby and realize that I owe this girl everything for keeping Cassidy alive. "Shelby, thank you so much for everything you did for Cassidy while she was in that place. I owe you more than I can ever say."

"You don't owe me anything. I just wish I could have protected her from that monster."

"There's nothing more you could have done, Shelby, and you know it. You're not allowed to be sad. I'm ok now," Cassidy says.

Shelby just nods. "We'll have to agree to disagree on that one."

"They never did anything to you, did they?" Austin asks Shelby.

She shakes her head and looks at the floor. "He drew a lot of blood from me and took other samples, but he never got the chance to auction me off for breeding. I think he was getting ready to, though. I lied to him about my age and told him I was only eighteen. He may have been a monster, but I don't think he wanted to be a part of statutory rape. I'm almost nineteen but I have the benefit of looking really young, so he didn't question it. I don't know what I would have done if he made me go to the battle room. I'm sure what happened between you and Cooper wasn't going to happen for me."

Austin growls at this and gets up to pace around. If I'm not mistaken, it seems like there may be something there between him and

Shelby. I keep catching each of them glancing at each other when they think no one is looking. I might have to push him on that one later.

We all sit and talk for a while. I try to steer the conversation away from everything that happened, but Cassidy keeps coming up with more questions. After about an hour, she starts to fade quickly.

"All right, everyone. I think we need to let Cassidy get some more rest," I say.

Everyone groans and complains, but eventually, we say good night and they both leave. I crawl up onto the bed with her and pull her into my arms.

"Cooper?"

"Yeah, baby."

"Thank you for coming for me."

"I will always come for you. I love you."

That night, we drift off to sleep together. Her, finally safe, and me, holding my life in my arms.

Chapter 23
Celebrations
Cassidy

I've been out of the hospital now for a few months. The interrogations with Anderson have finished and they transferred him to a maximum-security prison until his trial. The President made it his top priority to find Vice President Thompson. They found him after about a week, hiding in some remote cabin in Montana. Someone on his staff gave away his position because they didn't want to go to jail for protecting him. He is with Anderson at that prison awaiting his trial as well.

Cooper and Austin have been helping clear out the remaining facilities. He has had to go away for a couple of days here and there but when the President himself asks for your help, you don't say no. He was not happy to have to leave me, but I'm doing ok. I finished physical therapy on my hand, and it is almost back to normal. There are still times when it aches, but considering what they did to me, I'll take it. I have a huge scar on my arm where the one serum burned me. It bothers me only for the fact that every time I look at it, I think about that moment. I have taken to wearing long-sleeved shirts so I can't see it.

I started seeing one of the therapists here on base. We talk a couple of times a week about everything that I went through. When Cooper is here, he comes with me. I know that it is going to take a long time for me to fully recover, but I am really trying hard. I frequently have nightmares about my time with Anderson. I know he can't hurt me anymore, but that doesn't make all the memories go away. I wake up screaming a lot, but Cooper is there to help me. When he goes away, Shelby stays with me. I am pretty much never alone anymore, but I prefer it that way. When I am alone, I tend to get lost in my head, and right now, that's not the place that I want to be.

Cooper is meeting with the General and Colonel right now about their most recent mission. He and Austin had to go to Florida to close up one of the last facilities. They got back yesterday and have spent a lot of time in meetings since they returned.

Right now, I'm with Shelby, getting ready for something that I planned for Cooper as a surprise.

"How do I look?" I ask, twirling around for her.

"You look beautiful," she says, coming over to straighten my dress.

Shelby and I have been busy planning a wedding. Cooper asked me the day after I woke up and of course, I said yes. We decided that we would get married once I was healed, but with all his missions and meetings, there hasn't really been time. While he was away this last time, I met with Mike, uh, General McConnell, and asked him if we could do the wedding when Cooper got back. He, of course, said yes, and told me to let him know what I needed him to do. I wanted it to be a surprise for Cooper. He has done so much for me that I wanted to do something nice for him. We planned everything for today. We have the field behind the Administration building set up. Mike is going to marry us, and Austin is going to give me away. Shelby will be my maid-of-honor and Austin, who is in on everything, will be Cooper's best man.

The General asked the boys to come to the meeting today in their dress blues under the ruse that they were doing a teleconference with the President.

I don't know how he pulled it off, but Mike arranged for someone to bring me a wedding dress. It's nothing fancy, just a white silky slip dress, but it looks nice on me. My scar is showing, but for some reason, today I don't care. Shelby is wearing a simple lavender tea-length dress. Her hair is twisted up into an intricate updo, thanks to a woman on the base who used to be a hairdresser. My hair is down and curled at the ends. The same woman pulled one side of my hair up into a braid and made it look stunning.

Now that we are finally ready, we head down to wait in the field. Cooper should be done shortly, and Austin is bringing him directly to our setup.

I stand off to the side so that he won't see me right away. I can hear them talking and know that in just a few minutes, I will be walking down our makeshift aisle to marry my man.

"What is going on, Austin?" I hear Cooper ask. "I told Cassidy I would meet up with her as soon as we were done. I don't have time to mess around."

He sounds angry, which makes me laugh. When they turn the corner, Cooper immediately stops and looks around. Yup, we definitely surprised him. I am behind the corner of the building where he can't see me. But I am peeking around so that I can see his reaction.

"Welcome to your wedding," Austin says.

"My what? Where's Cassidy?" Cooper asks anxiously.

"Well, if you would just get your big, stupid ass down front, I will bring her to you," Austin teases him.

Cooper smiles and starts making his way toward the front. Austin comes over to where I am hiding and stops short. "You look stunning, kid," he says, kissing me on the cheek.

"Thanks, Aus. And thanks for helping me with the planning," I say.

Austin looks at me and smiles. "You know, Mom and Dad would be so proud of you. I know that even though they aren't here in person, they are both watching from above. I'm so proud to be able to give you away on your wedding day. So proud."

"Austin James Daniels, don't you dare make me cry today!"

He chuckles. "Come on, kids. Let's go get you married," he says, holding his arm out to me.

I loop my arm through his and we make our way to the end of the aisle. The second we step out Cooper's eyes are on me. He smiles so wide and puts his hand up to his chest. I smile back at him. I know there are a bunch of our friends from the base, but I just can't tear my eyes away from him. My man, my life, my heart.

Someone cues the music and Austin and I start our walk. Cooper stares at me the whole way. When we finally reach him, Austin hands me over and whispers something to Cooper, that makes him smile. I slide over to Cooper's arm, right where I belong.

Mike steps up in front of us and clears his throat. We turn to face him, and he begins. The ceremony is short and sweet. Cooper and I recite our vows and I cry the entire way through mine. Cooper sheds a tear or two as well. When Mike pronounces us man and wife, Cooper jumps on me. He dips me back and kisses the hell out of me. When he finally lets me up, I am out of breath, but it is the best feeling in the world.

We turn to the applause of our friends and make our way back down the aisle. When we get to the side of the building where I was originally hiding, Cooper pulls me into his arms.

"I can't believe you did this," he says, sounding astonished.

"I wanted to surprise you. And thank you," I say, laying my head on his chest.

"Why would you want to thank me?"

"Cooper, you have done so much for me since I met you. You have put me first over everything and taken care of me. I wouldn't be here right now if it weren't for you."

He cups my face with both of his hands and smiles. "Baby, you have no idea how much you mean to me, do you?"

"I know how much you mean to me," I say, leaning up to kiss his chin.

"Cass, everything I do, is for you. Since the moment that I first saw you, all those years ago, I knew that the only reason I was put on this Earth, was to take care of you. I will spend the rest of our lives proving that to you if I have to."

We spend the rest of the day and night, celebrating with our friends. There's dancing and pictures, lots of good food and laughter. But the best part of it all is there is hope. After everything that has happened, after all that we have been through, it is encouraging to see everyone relaxed and celebrating. We have lost so much, so many. We have all made sacrifices. But in the end, we stayed together. Not just Cooper, Austin, and I, but everyone. We came together and fought for what we believed in, for humanity. And we won. No one knows what the future holds. We just know that we will face it together.

I know I will most likely always have my nightmares. I will always have scarring, both physical and mental. But I also know that I will always have Cooper and Austin and the family that we have created here.

"So, what now?" I ask.

"Now, baby. We finally get to start our life together," he says, and he kisses me.

Yeah, I am definitely ok with that.

Thank you for reading my book. Please consider leaving a review. Independent authors like me depend on those reviews to spread the word.

Check out my website at www.wendyzuccauthor.com[1].

You can always reach me at wendyzuccauthor@gmail.com.

---

1. http://www.wendyzuccauthor.com

Don't miss out!

Visit the website below and you can sign up to receive emails whenever Wendy Zuccarello publishes a new book. There's no charge and no obligation.

https://books2read.com/r/B-A-TRVU-WPDFC

BOOKS 2 READ

Connecting independent readers to independent writers.

Did you love *Sacrifice*? Then you should read *Winter Must End*[2] by Wendy Zuccarello!

[3]

Skylar Forrester and Oliver Woodman did not have the typical, all-American childhood. No, these two grew up in a fallout shelter after the world was destroyed by nuclear war when they were only five years old. It is all they have ever known since neither of them has any memory of life before the world went to hell. Their friendship was the only thing that kept them sane.

Fifteen years after they entered the shelter, it erupts in chaos when riots ensue, and the doors to the shelter open for the first time. Sky and Oli have no choice but to leave the only life they have ever known. They leave behind safety, shelter, food, family... anything you can think of, for a life out in a ravaged world where danger lurks at every turn.

---

2. https://books2read.com/u/bP7GNR

3. https://books2read.com/u/bP7GNR

They stumble upon southern charmer Sebastian Attwood and form an unlikely trio. They travel in search of something, anything that will prove that life will go on. When romance blooms between Sky and Bastian, things get complicated, and relationships are strained. They not only have to battle for their lives, but for each other.

Follow Sky, Oli, and Bastian on their journey to see if they can survive the harsh reality that is in their new world. Can life go on after it is torn apart? Is love enough to save what they have?

This is a guaranteed HEA with a lot of action and adventure, love and romance, and possibly a few tears.

Read more at https://www.wendyzuccauthor.com/.

Also by Wendy Zuccarello

All in Due Time
Winter Must End
Guarding Gwyn
Silent Hero
Sacrifice
Viable
Chasing Freedom
The Only Time We Get
Loudening Silence

Watch for more at https://www.wendyzuccauthor.com/.

About the Author

Wendy Zuccarello lives in central New Jersey with her husband, two teenagers, and many pets. She has her MFA in Creative Writing. In her spare time, when she is not reading or writing, she enjoys watching movies with her family, photography, and baseball.

Read more at https://www.wendyzuccauthor.com/.

www.ingramcontent.com/pod-product-compliance
Lightning Source LLC
Chambersburg PA
CBHW052034150726

48002CB00002B/602